she said/she saw

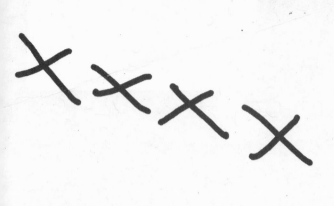

she said/she saw

Norah McClintock

ORCA BOOK PUBLISHERS

Library and Archives Canada Cataloguing in Publication

McClintock, Norah
She said/she saw / Norah McClintock.

Issued also in electronic format.
ISBN 978-1-55469-335-1

I. Title.
PS8575.C62S54 2011   JC813'.54   C2010-908039-4

First published in the United States, 2011
Library of Congress Control Number: 2010942099

Summary: When Tegan witnesses the murder of two friends, she must struggle
with people thinking she knows more than she is saying.

*Orca Book Publishers is dedicated to preserving the environment and has printed
this book on paper certified by the Forest Stewardship Council.*

Orca Book Publishers gratefully acknowledges the support for its publishing programs
provided by the following agencies: the Government of Canada through the Canada Book
Fund and the Canada Council for the Arts, and the Province of British Columbia through
the BC Arts Council and the Book Publishing Tax Credit.

Cover design by Teresa Bubela
Typesetting by Nadja Penaluna
Cover photo by Getty Images

ORCA BOOK PUBLISHERS
PO Box 5626, Stn. B
Victoria, BC Canada
V8R 6S4

ORCA BOOK PUBLISHERS
PO Box 468
Custer, WA USA
98240-0468

www.orcabook.com
Printed and bound in Canada.

14 13 12 11 • 4 3 2 1

ONE
Kelly

Two things I know:

One, everybody has a story to tell, and everybody tells their story in a different way. Me, I'm cinematic. I see life—my life, everyone's life—like a movie or a TV drama, or, sometimes, a comedy. My sister Tegan, on the other hand, sees her life like one of those big, fat, old-fashioned novels with herself as the tragic (or triumphant) heroine at the center of it all.

Two, nobody sees the whole story. Nobody can. There are always things in other people's heads that you can't know, not for sure, not even when other people tell you what they're thinking, because, let's face it, not everyone tells the truth. Sure, you can guess and maybe even get pretty close to the truth sometimes. But just as often, even more often, you're wrong. And I can guarantee you that almost all of the time there are pieces missing—the things that people are thinking to themselves that they would never say out loud, the things people don't even want to admit to themselves.

So, if you want to get the whole story (or as close to the whole story as is possible) about my sister Tegan— *Did she see or didn't she?*—you need to pull the pieces together and then take a good hard look at them and decide for yourself what's true and what isn't. That's what I had to do.

Here are the pieces.

TWO
Kelly

INT.—KELLY'S BEDROOM—DAY

KELLY TYRELL [that's me], 17, paces in a tight circle on the throw rug in her cluttered bedroom. The walls of the room are plastered with movie posters. The shelves are stuffed with videocassettes, DVDs and books, most of them about movies and writing screenplays. She is talking into a cell phone.

KELLY

What am I—my sister's keeper?

She turns to the camera as she listens to whatever the person on the other end is saying.

KELLY (CONT'D)
(to the camera)
Jeez, am I ever getting tired of the same questions over and over.
(into the phone)
I already told you—I don't know. I wasn't there. (pause) Right. Fine. Great talking to you too.

She snaps the phone shut.

KELLY (CONT'D)
(muttering)
Asshole.

She flings the cell phone onto the double bed that dominates the room and faces the camera again.

KELLY (CONT'D)
(to the camera)
What's wrong with people? Why do they think I'm supposed to know every detail of my sister's life just because we're "practically twins."
(making air quotes)
What does that even mean? You can't be *practically* twins any more than you can be *almost* unique.

Twinning is absolute, not relative. Well, you know what I mean. You either are a twin or you're not. Tegan and I are *not* twins. We were born in the same year, which, if you ask me, was bad planning on someone's part—Mom, are you listening? But we weren't born on the same day. We don't have that special bond that twins are supposed to have. We don't spend all of our time together. We don't have a special twin language. Most of the time, we don't even talk to each other. I'm not being bitchy or self-serving when I say that that's mostly Tegan's fault. She's the problem in our so-called relationship. She's always pulling the big-sister routine on me, like a ten-month lead makes her smarter or wiser or better than me. That's bull. I was potty-trained before her, for God's sake. Okay, so she gets better grades than me, most of the time without even trying.

She picks up a brush and starts to brush her hair in front of the mirror on her dresser.

KELLY (CONT'D)

She's prettier than me too. She looks a lot like Mom, whereas I take after our dad, who was one of those super-nice guys that everyone liked, especially the ladies, even though he was kind of plain and vertically challenged, not to mention follically challenged. But so what?

She glowers at the mirror and throws down the brush.

KELLY (CONT'D)

Tegan hangs out with a different crowd too, mostly kids a year ahead of us in school, and mostly, if you ask me, because she'd rather die than find herself in the same social circle as me. That's fine with me. Do you think I want to be around my snobby, bitchy big sister every hour of every day? It's bad enough being in so many of the same classes with her. Do you think I care if she wants to act all *I'm-way-cooler-than-you* and get off hanging out with guys like Clark Carson and Thomas Skelton, guys with too much money and even more attitude? Well, I don't. Besides, I have my own thing going. I swim. I'm good at it too. I have a wall of medals to prove it. I'd rather be in the pool where it's all real, where you make it based on what you can do, not on who your parents are and whether you can score booze and weed for your parties while your parents are out of town for the weekend.

A VOICE
(in the distance, muffled by the door)
Kel-ly! Time to set the table!

KELLY opens the door and sticks her head out.

KELLY
(shouting)
It's Tegan's turn!

THE VOICE
She isn't feeling well, so I told her she could lie down and we'd call her when supper was ready.

KELLY
(rolling her eyes and muttering to herself)
Of course.

She looks at the camera again.

KELLY (CONT'D)
For those of you who don't know my sister, congratulations are in order. But since you're going to meet her, there's something you should know. She's a

drama queen, a real diva-type personality. You know, one of those *the-earth-revolves-around-me* types. Everything that happens to her is therefore, by definition, phenomenally important. History in the making, right up there with presidential assassinations, superstar overdoses or the latest on the Obama kids. She records it all in her All About Me file on her computer, a running documentary on her oh-so-fascinating life that she inputs every night, and sometimes more often, depending on what earth-shattering event she happens to be at the center of. I used to ask her, "Why do you bother?"

DISSOLVE TO FLASHBACK:

INT.—TEGAN'S BEDROOM—NIGHT

TEGAN TYRELL, 17, is sitting at her desk, typing on her computer. One end of the room is filled with shelves that are stuffed with books. Instead of posters, there are framed reproductions of classic paintings on her wall. KELLY is in the open doorway, watching her sister.

KELLY

Who do you think is going to read all that crap?

TEGAN
(without looking up)
Samuel Pepys, Anaïs Nin…

KELLY
They're dead.

TEGAN
Susannah Moodie, Catherine Parr Traill.

KELLY
Also dead.

TEGAN
They're all regular people who kept diaries that are still being read decades, even centuries, later.

KELLY
Oh, so now you're a *regular* person?

TEGAN
People will be interested. Just you wait and see.

CUT BACK TO:
INT.—KELLY'S BEDROOM—DAY

A VOICE

Kelly! Everything's ready! Come on!

KELLY sighs as she steps out of her room. She looks into the camera as it precedes her down the stairs.

KELLY

I hate to admit it—you have no idea how much I hate it—but Tegan turned out to be right. For a while, there were people who would have loved to get their hands on that diary of hers—if they knew it existed. A lot of people who wanted to know the whole story, who wanted the answer to the million-dollar question: *Did she see or didn't she?*

THREE

Tegan

Just back from the police station. I still can't believe it. I can't believe any of it. And the cops—they give me the creeps.

This is what happened.

"I need to get everything clear in my mind, Tegan," Detective Zorbas said. He's an old man, in his mid-forties, stocky, with a good-sized paunch on him that makes you think it must be true what they say about cops. They really must have a special weakness for donuts. "I'd like you to tell me one more time what you saw."

One more time. One more time. It was always one more time. What was wrong with him? Why didn't he listen the first time?

"I already told you everything I know." If Kelly had been there, she would have given me that disapproving look of hers and accused me of using *that* tone of voice, the one she says makes her want to slap me because I sound like I have a pickle up my butt. But Detective Zorbas just nodded.

"I know," he said—as in, *I know that's what you said, but*...Why didn't he man up and tell me exactly what he was thinking: *But I don't believe you.*

But he didn't say that. Instead he said, "I know this is difficult, Tegan." He kept using my name, the way car salesmen do when they're working hard to build some kind of connection so they can sell people cars with accessories and extras they don't really want or aren't really interested in. "But you want us to catch whoever did this, don't you?"

See what I mean? Why would he ask that unless he thought I was holding out on him? Unless he thought I was hiding something or protecting someone? Unless he thought I wasn't being straight with him?

"Try to relax," he said.

Right. Like *that* was ever going to happen.

"Just take a deep breath and start from the beginning. Tell me everything you can remember, even if it doesn't seem important. Okay?"

I looked at my mother, who was sitting beside me and holding my hand. She stared back at me, her eyes more serious than I had ever seen them, like she was trying to tell me something: *Do the right thing. Say the right thing.*

There was no window in the cramped little interview room we were in. There was no air either. I had changed into some clothes my mother had brought from home, and I'd washed off as best I could after they let me. But even though it wasn't there anymore, I could still feel the blood that had splattered against my face, warm when it first hit me and then, later, cold, sticky, congealing. I felt other stuff too, stuff I'd reached up and touched, first wondering what it was and then screaming—or maybe just screaming louder—when I realized where it had come from.

Tell me one more time.

"Clark and Martin and I went to Thomas's place around nine," I said, as if I were reading out loud lines I'd had to write over and over on the blackboard as some kind of punishment. I wasn't telling Zorbas anything that he didn't already know or anything that I hadn't said a couple of times already—to the cops who arrived on the scene first, to Zorbas and his partner at the scene, to Zorbas and some other detective after they brought me to the police station to wait for my mother. "There were maybe ten other people there—you have all their names, you can check with them. Everybody was having a good time. And, yes, there was some drinking." That was one of the first things they had asked me about, only they hadn't really asked. It was more like they accused me, and I was so rattled, I blurted out the truth. I did it because— I would never admit this to anyone—I was afraid I was going to get into trouble for it, like it even mattered. "But Clark didn't drink anything except soda because he was driving," I said. Clark liked to party, but not when he was going to drive, not after what happened to his brother Scott, who hadn't been so smart and who was in a wheelchair now for the rest of his life.

"What about Martin?"

I looked him in the eye. "I think he had a couple of beers," I said. I'd said it at least three times already. "Everyone was mellow. Nobody got into a fight. Nobody argued. We were just playing computer games and listening to music—you know, celebrating the end of midterms."

Thomas had texted us all the first day of midterm exams: *Mark your calendars*. Thomas believed in working hard—he was going to get a scholarship to an Ivy League college if it killed him. But he also believed in rewarding all that work.

"We stayed until a little after midnight. The party was still going on, but Martin had practice the next day." Martin was the star of the school basketball team. He was so good that the coach kept after him about getting an athletic scholarship, but Martin wasn't interested. He said he wouldn't have time for competitive athletics after high school. He was going for pre-med. Martin wanted to be a doctor—but not some rich, fat specialist who lived the high life. No way. Martin wanted to practice in Africa, in countries where there were never enough doctors, never enough drugs, never enough hospitals; places where there wasn't enough peace either, where people were existing, not really living, in refugee camps.

Just thinking about him made me want to cry. Tears started to trickle down my cheeks. I didn't have the energy to wipe them away.

"You okay, Tegan?" Zorbas said. "You want me to get you some more water? A Coke?"

Like that would change anything. I just wanted to get this over with, go home and take a hot shower—maybe a couple of hot showers.

"Clark's car, his suv"—brand new, a Christmas present from his parents—"was parked about a block from Thomas's condo," I said. "The three of us walked to it together. I don't remember seeing anyone on the street, but that doesn't mean there wasn't anyone." I was walking between Clark and Martin. Martin was smiling and talking about a concert that was coming up. Besides basketball and medicine, he was big-time into music. I was waiting for him to ask me to go to the concert with him when he tripped on something. I grabbed him to stop him from falling, and he slipped an arm around my waist. He didn't let go even after he had regained his footing. I was sure now that Clark had just been teasing me earlier. He'd acted all weird, whispering in my ear whenever he caught me looking at Martin. *Forbidden fruit,* he'd said. *Forbidden fruit.* But would he tell me what that meant? No way. He'd just flash me a sly smile and say, *You'll find out soon enough.* Well, in case he hadn't noticed, Martin and I had been pretty tight all night—as tight as his arm was around my waist at that moment— and Martin hadn't acted like forbidden fruit. Instead, by the way he looked at me, I knew he wanted to ask me something, and I was pretty sure I knew what it was. I'd been waiting forever.

"Afraid you're going to slip and fall again?" I'd said, laughing, enjoying every second of physical contact with him.

"Okay, sure," he said with a goofy smile. "I guess that's as good an excuse as any to hold a drop-dead gorgeous babe."

I laughed, pretending he was just kidding around, but inside I felt warm and happy. I wished we'd never get to Clark's car because then maybe Martin's arm would be around my waist forever.

But I didn't tell Zorbas that. It was too personal and had nothing to do with anything that had happened.

"We got to the car. Clark got in behind the wheel. Martin opened the back door for me." I'd been hoping he'd get in with me and sit beside me and hold me all the way home. But he didn't. He got in the passenger seat up front, and Clark leaned over and whispered something to him. Martin shoved him away. He looked angry. I wanted to ask him what was going on, but I didn't think he'd tell me, not with Clark sitting there. So I kept my mouth shut. "Then Martin got in the front passenger seat. I still didn't see anyone else around."

I said that because the cops kept asking me: *Are you sure, Tegan? Are you sure you didn't see anyone?* I kept telling them the same thing: "I didn't see anyone. I was looking at Martin. He was digging through the CDs Clark kept in the car, trying to find something to play on the way home." I remembered his impish grin as he teased Clark for his terrible taste in music. Then Clark turned and gave him a look I couldn't decipher. Martin's cheeks turned pink. He glanced from Clark to me. Clark nodded at him, and Martin sighed. He turned to say something to me. But before he got a word out, his eyes shifted from me to, I think, the driver's-side window. *BOOM!*

BOOM!

BOOM!

"All of a sudden I heard a bang, and I saw Martin slump forward."

"Martin," Detective Zorbas said, as if he was hearing it for the first time. He frowned, just like he did every time I said it. "What about Clark? What was he doing?"

"I don't know. There was another bang right after that. Then another."

Something had stung my cheek. It turned out to be a shard of glass.

Something splattered all over my face and my hair and the front of my coat. It turned out to be blood and brains and tiny pieces of bone.

Someone screamed. It turned out to be me.

"But it was Martin who slumped over after the first shot?"

"Yes."

"You're sure of that?"

"Yes."

"Did you see who did it?"

God, was he ever going to actually *listen* to me?

"No," I said. "He must have taken off right after he fired the shots."

"He," Detective Zorbas said. "You keep saying that. You said 'he' to the first officers on the scene. You said 'he' to me at the scene. If you didn't see anything, how do you know it was a he?"

"I—" I shook my head. It was a good question. "It just felt like a he. I mean, that's usually how it turns out, right? When someone gets shot, it's almost always a guy who did it. Right?"

"Are you sure that's what it is? Are you sure you didn't see something—a hand, maybe—that made you think it was a male? Or maybe you peeked out the window while he was running away. Maybe you got an idea if he was tall or short, thin or stout. Maybe you saw if he was wearing a jacket or a coat, shoes or boots. Maybe you saw which direction he ran, if he was headed for a car or if he ducked down an alley. Anything you can tell us will help, Tegan."

"I didn't see him." Jeez, I'd said it again: *he*. It just kept coming out. "I mean, I didn't see anything. I didn't see anyone."

FOUR

Kelly

INT.—TYRELL LIVING ROOM—DAY

KELLY is standing in the middle of the living room in pajamas and Cookie Monster slippers. Her hair is tousled. She faces the camera.

> ### KELLY
>
> Tegan told her story to the police four times, not the "dozens of times" she whines about. She told Mom too. But did it occur to her to tell me? Of course not.

CUT TO:

INT.—TYRELL FOYER—DAY

The door opens. TEGAN and MRS. TYRELL enter.

MRS. TYRELL has her arm around her daughter, whose eyes are red from crying. KELLY rushes to the door.

                    KELLY
What happened? What did the cops want, Mom? Why didn't you call me?

                MRS. TYRELL
Not now, Kelly. We've been up all night. Tegan needs to get some rest.

                    KELLY
What happened, Teeg? Did the party get busted?

KELLY turns to the camera.

                KELLY (CONT'D)
It wouldn't surprise me. Those parties are drug central. It would serve them right if they all got busted.

                MRS. TYRELL
Not now, Kelly!

                    KELLY
Teeg?

                      21

> TEGAN
> (in a weary monotone)
Not now, Kelly.

MRS. TYRELL and TEGAN climb the stairs, leaving KELLY to stare after them.

CUT TO:
INT.—TYRELL LIVING ROOM—DAY
KELLY, still in her pajamas, continues to address the camera.

> KELLY
Tegan was too shaken up to tell me what happened. Too exhausted.

She throws an arm over her eyes and strikes a dramatic pose.

> KELLY (CONT'D)
Too traumatized.

She drops her arm and sighs.

KELLY (CONT'D)

I'm not as insensitive as she thinks I am. I know she was exhausted. I know she was traumatized. Who wouldn't be after a thing like that? She could have been killed. In fact, it's probably a miracle that she wasn't. The cops think it was the tinted windows that saved her. They think the killer didn't see her. But, still, she could have taken a few minutes to brief me. She could have told me herself what happened instead of letting me find out the hard way.

CUT TO:

INT.—TYRELL KITCHEN—DAY

KELLY, still in her pajamas and her Cookie Monster slippers, is sitting at the table pouring milk into a bowl of cereal.

KELLY

Jeez, what a family. Mom gets a call from the cops in the middle of the night. She races out of here. She's gone all night. Tegan, who went out, never comes home. But did it occur to either of them what I must have been thinking? Did anyone even think to call me? Have they told me what happened yet? No, they're upstairs together. Tegan is crying. Ten to one, she got busted.

A radio is on, and a newscast begins. KELLY gets up and reaches to turn the radio off but suddenly freezes.

NEWS READER'S VOICE

...Dead are Clark Carson and Martin Genovese, both eighteen, both students at Lakeside Collegiate. Police are investigating but so far have no motive for the shooting. Sources say there was a third person in the car at the time of the shooting, but police have not released that person's name. The investigation continues. Turning to other news...

KELLY stares at the radio. Her face is pale. She reaches out slowly and shuts the radio off. She stares at the ceiling above her. Then she gets up and heads for the kitchen door.

KELLY
(shouting)

Mom!

FIVE
Kelly

INT.—TYRELL LIVING ROOM—DAY

KELLY is curled up in an armchair in front of the window. A textbook is open on her lap, but she does not look at it. Instead, she is staring, glassy-eyed, through the living room and the dining room beyond and out the window into the backyard. She is jarred out of her thoughts when the doorbell rings. She makes a move to get up, but before she can rise, her mother bustles out of the kitchen. KELLY hears the front door open. She hears voices.

MAN'S VOICE

Mrs. Tyrell? My name is Tony Genovese. Martin's father.

MRS. TYRELL
(sounding breathless and nervous)
Mr. Genovese, I'm so sorry for your loss.

KELLY
(to herself)
What does he want?

MR. GENOVESE
Thank you. I was wondering, Mrs. Tyrell, if I could speak to your daughter.

There is a long pause, and KELLY leans forward in the chair, straining to hear.

MRS. TYRELL
Tegan? She's...Of course. Of course. Please come in, Mr. Genovese.

MR. GENOVESE
Please, call me Tony.

MRS. TYRELL
Louise. Please come in. I'll go and get Tegan.

MR. GENOVESE and MRS. TYRELL appear in the doorway to the living room. MR. GENOVESE is a short, wiry man dressed in black chinos and a sport jacket. He looks weary. MRS. TYRELL, by contrast, looks nervous and jumpy.

MRS. TYRELL
Please sit down. I'll be right back.

MR. GENOVESE enters the living room. MRS. TYRELL disappears up the stairs. MR. GENOVESE is halfway to the sofa when, startled, he notices KELLY sitting in the armchair at the window. KELLY stands up, embarrassed.

KELLY
I'm Kelly. Tegan's sister. I knew Martin. I'm sorry about what happened.

MR. GENOVESE'S eyes tear up. KELLY, even more embarrassed now, starts to sit down but seems to change her mind. She remains standing. She and MR. GENOVESE look at each other. Neither seems at ease. MR. GENOVESE looks over his shoulder at the stairs. Footsteps are heard off-camera. KELLY breathes a sigh of relief and sinks back down into her chair.

SIX

Tegan

After what happened, I didn't want to talk to anybody. I didn't even want to leave my room. But things never work out the way I want. Never.

The day after it all happened, my mother knocked on the door to my room. She pushed it open and poked her head inside, even though I told her to go away.

"Martin's father is here," she said.

My stomach tied itself into a knot. I had met Mr. Genovese a couple of times. He was a contractor, a real success story. He had started out as a common laborer after dropping out of high school at sixteen to help support his family. He was smart, Martin said, but he wasn't book-smart. He was street-smart, money-smart, people-smart. According to Martin, his dad had worked sixteen-hour days the whole time Martin was growing up. It had paid off. Martin's family lived in the best neighborhood in the city, in a house that Mr. Genovese had built himself. There were five kids—four girls and Martin. It had always been Mr. Genovese's dream that Martin would come into the business with him and eventually take it over. But Martin had other ideas. Mr. Genovese was disappointed, but just a little.

"He likes the idea that I'm going to be the first Genovese to go to university," Martin told me. "He *really* likes the idea that I want to be a doctor. But, boy, he doesn't understand why I don't want to be a rich specialist. He doesn't understand me. But..." Martin always shrugged when he got to that part. If you ask me, he was exactly like his dad: he was enormously proud of what his dad had accomplished, but he didn't understand him any more than his dad understood him.

Now Martin was dead. I didn't think I could face Mr. Genovese and his grief.

"What does he want?" I asked my mother.

"He says he wants to talk to you."

I felt like I was going to throw up.

"What did you tell him?"

"I said I would come and get you. What else could I say? That poor man, Tegan."

"Can't you tell him I'm asleep?"

"I know how you feel, honey—"

No, she didn't. She absolutely didn't. She had no idea how I felt.

"Tell him I took a sleeping pill and you don't know when I'll wake up. Tell him—"

"You have to talk to him, Tegan. It's the least you can do."

The *least* I could do? What did she mean by that? Did she think there was something *more* I could do? Something more I could have done?

"I'll put on some coffee. I'll tell him you'll be right down," my mother said. She closed the door softly and floated down the carpeted hall and the carpeted stairs.

I sat up in bed, but it seemed like half a lifetime before I swung my feet over the side, and another whole lifetime before I stood up. I was wearing sweatpants and a ragged old sweatshirt that should have gone into the Goodwill bag three seasons ago. I thought about changing into something else. Then I thought,

What's the point? Who cares what I'm wearing?
Mr. Genovese wouldn't even notice.

Mr. Genovese was neatly dressed in black slacks, a white
shirt and a charcoal-gray sports jacket. He wasn't wearing a
tie—Martin said he only ever wore one for weddings and
funerals—but he looked professional anyway. His shoes
looked either brand-new or freshly polished. His thick
hair, flecked with gray, sat neatly in place above his closely
shaved face. He had bags under his eyes, which were glazed
from lack of sleep. He stood up when I entered the living
room. My mom was there too, setting a tray on the coffee
table. So was Kelly. I glowered at her. Why didn't mom
shoo her away? Mr. Genovese had come to see me, not
her. I looked pointedly from her to the stairs, but before
she could take a hint, Mr. Genovese started talking to me.

"Tegan," he said. The warmth and sympathy in his
voice overwhelmed me. I thought he would be angry
with me because of what had happened. And because I
was still alive. "Thank you for agreeing to see me. I know
how hard this must be for you."

His tone was so gentle that I felt like crying. No
wonder Martin adored him.

"Please sit down," he said, as if I were in his living room instead of the other way around. He waited until my mother had poured us each a cup of coffee. "I had to talk to you, Tegan," he said. "Martin spoke of you so often. I know you were special to him."

Special? Any other time, under any other circumstances, I would have been thrilled to hear that and to know that Martin had actually talked to his father about me. The way Mr. Genovese talked, I knew Gina was wrong. For as long as I could remember, I'd been just Tegan, one of the gang, someone he'd known for years, a non-flowering shrub in his daily landscape. But now it looked like I'd been right and that Martin had finally started to feel about me the way I'd been feeling about him.

"The police told me you were with Martin when it happened."

That was all it took for my eyes to cloud with tears.

"I'm sorry," he said. He leaned across the coffee table and took my hands in his. His fingers were long and spidery, just like Martin's, but they were calloused, not smooth and soft. He held my hands firmly until I got my tears under control. Then he let go and sat back again, his sorrow-filled eyes on my own. "The police said you were in the backseat of Clark's car. They said—" His voice broke.

He shook his head slowly. "I need you to tell me what you saw, Tegan."

And there it was—the thing he'd come for. The thing I couldn't give him.

It took me a few moments before I could swallow the lump in my throat and say, "I didn't see anything, Mr. Genovese. I'm so sorry."

His eyes held mine, the sorrow in his eyes now transformed to a steely determination to get at the truth. I don't know why, but I suddenly pictured him staring down a supplier who was trying to pass off inferior products.

"I had a long talk with the head of the homicide squad, Tegan. He explained a lot of things to me. He told me, not that he needed to, how terrifying it can be to witness something as horrific as what you witnessed."

"Mr. Genovese—"

"He said that when something like that happens, most people tend to react the same way. They tend to think of themselves and their own safety. They wonder: am I going to die too? Am I next? He said people have described it to him as freezing up. Some people have told him that they're aware they're doing it—they feel themselves freezing even when their brain is telling them they should be doing something else: running, screaming, fighting back, anything except just sitting there waiting to be the next victim. But they can't help it. They're in shock. Their systems shut down, at least for a while. He says it's a perfectly normal reaction. It's nothing to be ashamed of."

Nothing to be ashamed of? What did that mean? What was he implying? Did he think *I* was ashamed?

"I've never been in your position, Tegan. But I understand people. That's one of the reasons I'm where I am now. I can read people. I know what they want and what they're afraid of. It sounds silly, I know, but people who are building a house, or renovating one, have a lot of fears—is the contractor honest, have they made the right choice, will they be cheated? I understand that. So I think I understand as much as anyone can who wasn't directly involved in...what you experienced...how it must have felt, what it must have been like. But this detective I spoke to, the head of the homicide squad, he told me that when the shock starts to wear off and people have time to think and to process what happened, they often remember something. It might not be something big or important. But he said that even the smallest thing, the seemingly most insignificant thing, can help."

His eyes hadn't left mine for even a moment. He continued to stare at me, waiting for me to say something like, *Well, now that you mention it, there was this one thing…*

"I didn't see anything, Mr. Genovese. I'm sorry."

Impatience flashed in his eyes. His jaw stiffened. But his voice remained calm and soothing.

"I know that's what you think, Tegan. I'm just asking you to concentrate for a minute. Maybe close your eyes. I know it's hard, but if you could just put yourself back in that vehicle…"

Close my eyes? Put myself back in that vehicle? He *knew* that was hard?

"I didn't see anything." I was fighting back anger, and I hated myself for it. He had lost his son. His only son. "I was looking at Martin. He was in a good mood, you know? So he was fooling around, and I was looking at him. Then it just happened." *BOOM! BOOM! BOOM!* Louder than I ever would have thought possible. "I didn't see anything."

Mr. Genovese sat across from me, his eyes never wavering, waiting for more, waiting for a miracle. But there wasn't any more. I wasn't an angel or a saint. I couldn't give him a miracle.

35

SEVEN
Kelly

INT.—TYRELL LIVING ROOM—DAY

KELLY watches her mother walk Mr. Genovese to the front door. She glances at TEGAN, who is sitting on her chair as if she had been poured out of a cement truck and had hardened into place. She listens as the front door opens and closes again and her mother walks past the living room into the kitchen.

> KELLY
> You could have told him you'd at least think about it. That's all he was asking.

At first TEGAN doesn't move. Then her eyes seem to click into focus.

> TEGAN
>
> And you could have minded your own business. He came here to see me, not you. And, for your information, I don't have to think about it. I know what I saw.

KELLY stares at her sister, trying to decode her last sentence.

> TEGAN (CONT'D)
>
> Everybody keeps asking me the same questions, and I keep giving them the same answers, and they still ask me, like I'm hiding something.

> KELLY
> (to the camera)
> Nobody had said that—not yet, anyway.

> TEGAN
>
> The police are the ones who are supposed to solve murders, not me. Why don't they do their jobs and leave me alone? Why don't they gather evidence and look for other witnesses?

                         KELLY

Other witnesses? What other witnesses?

TEGAN stands abruptly.

                         TEGAN

I'm going upstairs.

KELLY watches her go. She turns to the camera again.

                         KELLY

What other witnesses?

CUT TO:

INT.—HIGH SCHOOL HALLWAY—DAY

The hallway is crowded with teenaged students unpacking their backpacks into their lockers, catching up on gossip and clowning around before classes start for the day. KELLY is at her locker. An attractive blond girl is standing beside her. She is LACEY STRATTON, Kelly's best friend. KELLY, who has been stuffing textbooks and binders onto the top shelf of her locker, pauses to look angrily at another student, a girl.

KELLY

(to the girl)

Get lost, why don't you? It's none of your business.

LACEY

(also to the girl)

Yeah, get lost.

The GIRL glowers at them, spins around and marches a few paces down the hall, where she joins a group of girls and proceeds to whisper something to them. They all stare at Kelly.

KELLY

Jeez, if one more person asks me about Tegan, I *am* going to go postal.

(to the camera)

Mom let Tegan stay home today—post-traumatic stress disorder and all that. But what about me? Did anyone give even one second's thought to how stressful it would be to have a couple of hundred kids in your face, all trying to pump you for juicy gossip, all wanting to know *Is it true? Was she really there?* And, of course, the big one, *Did she see?*

39

KELLY shoves the last textbook into her locker and slams the door shut.

LACEY

I heard my mom tell my dad that she overheard Clark's parents talking while she was over there working with Scott.

KELLY

(to the camera)

Lacey's mom is a physiotherapist. She's been working with Clark's brother, Scott, ever since his accident.

LACEY

They've hired someone to look into what happened. Some kind of PI.

KELLY

(surprised)

Don't they trust the cops to find the killer?

LACEY

I guess not. You know what my mom said? Mr. Carson is used to giving orders and being in charge.

She said it's probably driving him nuts having to wait to hear from the cops. And you know cops—there's only so much they'll tell you.

LACEY peers at Kelly and bites her lip. She glances around the crowded hallway and steps in closer to Kelly.

LACEY (CONT'D)

My mom also said she heard Mr. Carson mention Tegan.

KELLY

What did he say?

LACEY

He was telling someone that Tegan knew Clark and that she was in the car when it happened. Did she say anything to you, Kelly? Did she see anything?

KELLY
(sighing)

I don't know. She won't talk to me. But you know how she felt about Martin. If she saw anything, I'm pretty sure she would have said something.

41

> LACEY

Pretty sure?

> KELLY

You know what I mean.

> LACEY

What if Martin talked to her?

> KELLY

What?

> LACEY

What if Martin talked to her? What if he told her? (pause) Did he, Kel? Did he say anything to her?

> KELLY

Not that I know of.
> (to the camera)
She would have been all over me if he'd said anything. Talk about drama! She would have ripped out hair, shredded clothing—mine, of course, not hers.

LACEY peers into the distance, chewing her lower lip. KELLY stares at her, frowning.

SHE SAID / SHE SAW

KELLY (CONT'D)

What?

LACEY

Huh?

KELLY

There's something you're not telling me.

LACEY

No there isn't.

KELLY

Yes there is. I know you, Lacey. I've known you since third grade, and you were never a good liar.

LACEY

It's just…I thought…You told me Martin said he was quitting—smoking, I mean.

KELLY
(to the camera)

It's how the whole thing started between me and Martin—with me giving Martin a piece of my mind about his smoking—and I don't mean cigarettes.

43

DISSOLVE TO FLASHBACK:

INT.—HIGH SCHOOL GYMNASIUM—DAY

The gym has been set up with booths and information tables. Each one represents a different nonprofit organization, charity or community group. A huge banner hangs from the ceiling: *Get Involved, Make a Difference in Your Community*. Students are walking listlessly from table to booth to table, most of which are staffed by adults. KELLY wanders up and down the aisles between tables, looking bored and cranky. Then something catches her eye. She stares at a good-looking young man at the Doctors Without Borders table. He is MARTIN GENOVESE. A sort of smirk takes over her face. She walks toward him.

> KELLY
>
> Well, if it isn't the future Doctor Genovese. I'm surprised to see you here. According to this—

She holds up a small booklet entitled *The Students' Guide to Community Service: Fulfilling Yourself While Fulfilling Your Curriculum Requirement.*

> KELLY (CONT'D)
>
> —these groups screen their volunteers pretty carefully. They even do police checks.

MARTIN
(grinning at her)
That's only when you work with vulnerable popula-
tions, like children and seniors.

KELLY
Good thing for you, I guess. I mean, what would they
think if they found out you were a pothead?

MARTIN
What I do on my own time—

KELLY
And that you got busted.

MARTIN grabs Kelly by the arm and hauls her to the
side of the gym. When he speaks, he drops his voice
and glances around to make sure no one can hear
him.

MARTIN
What are you talking about?

KELLY
Like you don't know. Look, what you do is your

business, but you hang around with my sister. How do I know you don't—

MARTIN

What makes you think I ever got busted?

KELLY

I heard *your* sister talking about it.

MARTIN's face turns pale.

KELLY (CONT'D)

She doesn't know I heard her. She was in the girls' washroom. She thought she was alone. She was on her cell phone. I think she might have been talking to you.

MARTIN

Did she say anything to anyone about it?

KELLY

Not that I know of. But I don't know your sister all that well.

MARTIN

What about you? Did you tell anyone? Did you tell Tegan?

KELLY

No.

MARTIN

So she doesn't know?

KELLY

If she does, she didn't hear it from me.

MARTIN breathes a sigh of relief.

KELLY (CONT'D)

She keeps telling me how you want to be some do-gooder doctor, helping people in all those countries where there's starvation or civil wars going on or where AIDS is rampant. What kind of example are you going to set, huh?

MARTIN

They ended up letting me go. There were no charges.

                    KELLY

Right. So you're in the clear. There's nothing to worry
about.
                (she shakes her head)
Stuff like that catches up with you, Martin.

She turns and walks away.

CUT TO:

INT.—HIGH SCHOOL HALLWAY—DAY

KELLY is walking past the gymnasium. She has a backpack slung over one shoulder. She is on her way out of
school. The door to the gym is open. Inside, people are
cleaning up after the volunteer fair. MARTIN is one of
those people. He spots Kelly and hurries out to her.

                    MARTIN

Hey, Kelly!

KELLY turns to face him.

                MARTIN (CONT'D)

Can I talk to you?

KELLY

About what?

MARTIN

About what you said.

KELLY

I really don't care what you do with your life, Martin.

MARTIN

Tegan told me you say exactly what's on your mind. She made it sound like a bad thing, but you know what? It's not so bad.

KELLY eyes him suspiciously.

MARTIN (CONT'D)

I want to explain—

KELLY

You don't have to.

She starts to circle around him, but he blocks her path.

MARTIN

I got off. Clark called his dad and his dad called some high-powered lawyer he knows, and they let me go with a warning. They didn't even tell my parents.

KELLY

Good for you.

MARTIN

The deal was, I had to do a program. And I did. I did the program. I haven't touched anything in five months now. And you know what? I'm glad. I can focus better. I feel better. More righteous, you know?

KELLY

Are you sure you don't mean more self-righteous?

MARTIN stares at her. She offers a smile. He smiles too.

KELLY (CONT'D)

Can I ask *you* something?

MARTIN nods.

KELLY (CONT'D)

Why did you ask if Tegan knew about your bust?

MARTIN

It's nothing. Really.

KELLY peers at him.

KELLY

You're a terrible liar.

MARTIN

She's my friend.

KELLY peers at him a few beats longer.

KELLY

I know she smokes up. I don't think my mom's figured it out. But I did. Ages ago. So if that's what you mean—

For a moment MARTIN says nothing. He studies Kelly.

MARTIN

Yeah, that's what I mean.

51

KELLY frowns. She knows there is more than what he is saying, but she can't figure out what.

MARTIN (CONT'D)

The thing I wanted to tell you, though—I quit. I learned my lesson. I did the program. I'm clean. One hundred percent drug-free. And I plan to stay that way.

KELLY

Great.

They stare at each other for a moment. KELLY is the first to break eye contact.

KELLY (CONT'D)

Unless there's anything else...

MARTIN says nothing. KELLY circles around him and bounds out the main door of the school.

CUT BACK TO:

INT.—HIGH SCHOOL HALLWAY—DAY

KELLY and LACEY are standing in front of Kelly's locker. The knot of girls down the hall are still staring at them.

KELLY

Martin quit that stuff. I know he did. Why?

LACEY

It's just that I heard...

LACEY shifts uncomfortably.

KELLY

For God's sake, Lacey, just spit it out. What did you hear?

LACEY

I heard he smoked up that night. Tegan too. I heard Clark's parents are making a big deal of it.

KELLY

No way. He quit. And Tegan...

KELLY frowns.

CUT TO:

INT.—TYRELL FOYER—NIGHT

TEGAN comes through the front door and throws her backpack onto the floor. KELLY is coming down the stairs.

TEGAN

I don't know what's gotten into Martin. He used to be fun. Now he says he doesn't want to party as much anymore. I don't get it.

CUT TO:

INT.—HIGH SCHOOL HALLWAY—DAY

KELLY and LACEY are still in front of Kelly's locker.

LACEY

I'm telling you what I heard from someone who was at the party. They were smoking up. Tegan *and* Martin.

A school bell rings. Locker doors slam up and down the hallway, and kids start to move to their first class of the day. KELLY stares at Lacey as if she can't believe what she has just heard.

LACEY (CONT'D)

Come on, Kel. You know how Austen gets if anyone comes to class late.

KELLY still doesn't move. LACEY grabs her by one arm and drags her down the hall.

EIGHT

Tegan

I stayed in my room all day Monday, dreading the moment when the doorbell would ring and Clark's parents would show up to ask the same questions as Mr. Genovese.

But they didn't come. Instead, a man named Mr. Deacon did, and, don't you know it, my mother, who had stayed home from work even though I told her she didn't have to (I wanted to be alone), let him into the house. Then she made me go downstairs and talk to him. He was a tall, handsome man in an expensive-looking navy-blue suit. His hand engulfed mine when he shook it.

"Mr. and Mrs. Carson asked me to drop by," he said. "I'd like to ask you some questions, Tegan, if that's okay with you."

No, it wasn't okay with me. But before I could say anything, my mother was fluttering around him like he was datable material.

"Please, come into the living room, Mr. Deacon," she said. "Can I make you some coffee?"

"No, thank you, Mrs. Tyrell." He sounded polite, but there was something cold behind his eyes. "I'm fine."

We sat down, me in the same armchair Kelly had sat in when Mr. Genovese had stopped by, my mother in the matching armchair next to me, and Mr. Deacon on the sofa on the other side of the coffee table. My mother clasped her hands in her lap and smiled nervously.

"Tegan, as I'm sure you can imagine, Mr. and Mrs. Carson are devastated by what happened," Mr. Deacon said.

"We all are," my mother said.

Mr. Deacon smiled pleasantly at her, but he didn't fool me. His smile was as fake as his politeness. My mother's hands tightened in her lap.

"They are even more devastated by the impasse the police find themselves in," Mr. Deacon continued.

"A senseless double homicide committed
infested part of the city, but in a good
filled with well-educated, hard-working p
people—and the police don't have a single lead. They
have the bullet casings, but no weapon. There are no
fingerprints. No footwear impressions. No hairs, no
fibers, no blood except the victims'."

I flinched when he said that. He was looking straight
at me. He knew the effect his words were having on me.
But that didn't stop him.

"The police have no idea who would have wanted
to kill those two boys, or why," he said. "They've talked to
Clark's and Martin's families. They've talked to both
boys' friends. They all say the same thing—that the boys
didn't have any enemies, that they weren't in any trouble,
that they hadn't been in any fights or arguments with
anyone. If anyone held some kind of grudge against
either of them, no one seems to know about it. The
police have nothing to go on, Tegan. And that means
that they're not likely to make any progress in finding
out who murdered these two fine boys."

I couldn't look him in the eyes. I just couldn't. Instead
I stared at his knees and at the sharp crease in his trousers,
and I waited.

"The only thing they do have, Tegan"—Here it comes, I thought—"is you."

"Tegan has already told the police everything she knows," my mother said.

"I understand that the police have interviewed her a couple of times." Mr. Deacon reached into his suit jacket, pulled out a couple of pieces of paper that were as crisp as the pale-blue shirt he was wearing. He unfolded them. "That's what I wanted to talk to you about, Tegan. There are a few things that I don't understand and a few questions I'd like to ask."

I felt sick again. This was never going to stop. People were going to keep on asking me and asking me, and every time they did, I saw Martin again. I saw his head explode.

"Let's start with the questions, why don't we?" He didn't seem to want an answer from me, or if he did, he didn't wait for one. "Now, I understand that you and Clark and Martin left school together on the day in question."

The day in question. He sounded like a cop or a lawyer. Come to think of it, he looked like a lawyer too, in his dark suit and silk tie.

"Is that right, Tegan?"

I nodded.

"But you didn't arrive at Thomas Skelton's condo until a little after nine PM. Is that right?"

I nodded again.

"What did the three of you do in the five and a half hours between the time you left school and the time you arrived at Thomas's condo?"

"Nothing," I said. I don't know how he meant it, but it sounded like he was accusing me of something. "We didn't do anything."

"What I mean, Tegan," Mr. Deacon said calmly, "is where did the three of you go?"

"To Martin's house. We went to Martin's house."

"Was anyone else there?"

Why was he asking that? What was he trying to get at?

"No."

"Just you and Clark and Martin?"

"Yes."

"What did you do at Martin's house?"

"Nothing. I mean, nothing special. We had something to eat. We watched some TV. We talked." I'd stared at Martin practically the whole time. I couldn't help it. I couldn't seem to stop looking at him. "Then we went to Thomas's."

"Did you do any drugs?"

"What?" My mother looked sharply at me. "Are you saying those boys took drugs?"

"No!" How dare he say that in front of my mother!

"Did you ever do drugs? I mean, did Martin or you ever do drugs?"

I looked at the papers in his hand. The cops had almost certainly done a postmortem by now. Had they run some kind of test for drugs? Is that how he knew?

I shook my head.

Mr. Deacon stared deep into my eyes. "That's not true, is it, Tegan?" he said. "You were high at the party that night, weren't you?"

I said nothing. Who did he think he was?

"You can lie to me, Tegan," Mr. Deacon said. "But I guarantee the police are going to ask you the same question, and it's a serious matter to lie to them."

Why was he here? Why didn't he go away?

"Tegan?" he said.

My mother's head was turned toward me. I felt her stare.

"Is this true, Tegan?" she said, tense now, as if Mr. Deacon, a complete stranger, had presented her with evidence that I was some kind of drug addict.

"It was just a little weed," I said to Mr. Deacon. I didn't look at my mother. I couldn't.

"You mean marijuana?" Mr. Deacon said.

"You took *drugs*?" My mother's voice was shrill.

"There was a joint going around. I took a few puffs."

"Tegan, how could you?" Her tone was one-half horror, one-half profound disappointment, as if I'd been caught mainlining heroin.

"What about Martin?" Mr. Deacon said.

"I don't know." It would have been better if I could have looked him in the eye when I answered, but I couldn't. "I didn't watch him all night."

"Did Martin ever do drugs?"

It was one thing to confess for myself. But there was no way I was going to make Martin look bad. "I don't know."

"But he did drugs that night, didn't he?"

"I already told you—I don't know."

"He did drugs that night, Tegan," he said, telling me now, not asking me. "What about Clark? Did he ever do drugs? And I'd appreciate your honesty this time, Tegan. So would his parents."

I stole a glance at my mother. I'd never seen her look so disappointed.

"Sometimes," I said.

"As often as you and Martin?"

What was he driving at?

"No." Clark preferred vodka to weed.

"Did Clark do any drugs recently that you know of?"

"No." Clark had sworn off drugs because of the accident. "At least, not that I know of."

"When you did drugs, where did you get them?" Mr. Deacon asked.

"It wasn't *drugs*." Jeez, he made it sound worse than it was. "It was *weed*."

He stared at me for a moment. "You can call it whatever you want, Tegan. But you are aware that marijuana is a prohibited substance, aren't you? You are aware that it's illegal?"

I stared right back at him.

"Where did you get the drugs, Tegan?"

"Where did *I* get them?" Now he was making me out to look bad. "It wasn't me. It was Martin—" I stopped. This man, this complete stranger, was accusing me of something. Now I was accusing Martin. Betraying him.

"It was Martin what?" Mr. Deacon said. "It was Martin who got the drugs when you needed them?"

"We didn't *need* them. It was just for fun, just to relax. That's all."

"Where did he get the drugs?"

"I don't know."

"He had a dealer he used, didn't he?"

"I said, I don't know!"

"Don't know or won't tell?"

"Mom!" I looked pleadingly at her. For a moment she sat motionless. She was angry with me. I had no choice. I started to cry. My mother took the hint. She stood up.

"I think you should leave," she told Mr. Deacon.

Mr. Deacon stayed where he was. His eyes stayed on me.

"Did you see Martin's drug dealer that night?" he said. "Did Martin get into some kind of dispute with him? Did he refuse to pay him? Is that what happened? Is that why Martin and Clark died?"

"No."

"No? So you *do* know something about this, don't you, Tegan?"

"No. I don't know anything."

"And yet you seem certain that Martin's drug dealer didn't shoot Martin and Clark?"

"That's not what I meant."

"According to the evidence and to what you told the police, the shooter was on the driver's side, isn't that right?"

I looked at my mother. Why didn't she make him go away?

"Tegan?" Mr. Deacon said.

"Yeah. So?"

"Don't you think it's odd that he was on Clark's side of the car but that he shot Martin first? Why do you think he did that?"

I just stared at him.

"What's the matter? Are you afraid, Tegan? Is that why you won't cooperate with the police?"

What?

"I told them everything I know."

"Did you?"

My mother stood up again.

"I want you to leave. Right now," she said.

"I'll understand if you tell me you're afraid, Tegan. The police can protect you. If you help them catch the scumbag who killed Clark and Martin, they'll protect you."

"I didn't see *anything*." How many times did I have to say it?

"You're upsetting my daughter." What she really meant was he was upsetting *her*. "If you don't leave immediately, I'll call the police."

Mr. Deacon stood up, but his eyes never left mine. "Or maybe it was one of Martin's dissatisfied customers," he said in a soft voice, like a snake's hiss. "Is that it, Tegan? Did Martin stiff one of his customers, maybe pass off some inferior stuff or shortchange someone? Is that what happened?"

"Martin didn't have customers."

"Are you sure about that? A lot of users deal on the side."

"He wasn't a user."

He glanced at the paper in his hands. "He smoked marijuana that night, Tegan. According to Thomas Skelton, so did you. Thomas said that Martin provided the marijuana. He was dealing, wasn't he?"

I stood up. I pushed him, hard. I didn't stop pushing him until he was out of the living room and in the front hall. He looked calmly at me.

"You really should cooperate with the police, Tegan. You should do the right thing. Clark is the innocent one here. He didn't deserve to die."

Clark didn't deserve to die? *Clark* was the innocent one? What was he saying—that Martin did deserve it?

He opened the door and was gone. I slammed the door behind him and turned. My mother was standing behind me.

"He's right, Tegan," she said. "If you know anything, you should tell."

NINE

Kelly

INT.—TYRELL FOYER—NIGHT

KELLY bursts through the front door, flinging down her backpack.

> KELLY
> (shouting)
> Tegan! Tegan, are you here?

> TEGAN
> (from the living room)
> I'm in here.

CUT TO:

INT.—TYRELL LIVING ROOM—NIGHT

TEGAN is curled up on the sofa when KELLY charges into the room, her face twisted in rage.

> KELLY
>
> How could you? And don't bother denying it! I know it was your fault!

> TEGAN
>
> Deny what? What are you talking about?

> KELLY
>
> Martin. He quit smoking dope, but he was smoking that night. Everyone says so. It was you, wasn't it? You pressured him into it!

> TEGAN
>
> (squirming uncomfortably)
> Obviously he didn't quit if he was smoking that night. And how dare you blame me! I'm under enough pressure as it is. Martin wouldn't have done anything he didn't want to do.

                    KELLY

He would if you nagged him enough. I know you.
You make such a pain of yourself that it's easy to do
whatever it is you want just to shut you up.

                    TEGAN
            (pulling herself up straight)
I don't know what you're talking about. And this is
none of your business. You weren't there. You have no
idea what happened, no idea what I went through.
Martin was my…he was my boyfriend.

                    KELLY
                (stunned)
What? Says who?

                    TEGAN
Says Martin.

                    KELLY
When?

                    TEGAN
At the party. Don't look so surprised. Martin and

I were friends forever. We hung out together. It just naturally evolved into something...more meaningful.

                         KELLY
You're lying!

                         TEGAN
                 (springing to her feet)
No, I'm not. We made it official that night. And then...
                 (her eyes tearing up)
And then that had to happen.

                         KELLY
Right—you finally got yourself a boyfriend and then someone had to come along and mess that up for you by shooting him. For your information—

KELLY suddenly clamps her mouth shut and draws in a deep breath.

                         TEGAN
                 (glowering at her)
I hate you, you know that? I absolutely hate you!

TEGAN runs out of the living room. Her footsteps are heard on the stairs, followed by a door slamming from somewhere up above. The camera moves in for an extreme close-up of Kelly.

KELLY
If I was a different kind of person, I'd tell her. I'd just come right out and tell her. But what good would it do, especially now?

She flops down onto the sofa and begins to cry softly.

TEN
Tegan

Jesus, my sister is a pain in the butt. Can't she see how I feel? Can't she understand what I'm going through? Two people were killed right in front of me. It's a miracle I wasn't killed myself. Every time I close my eyes, I see the scene again—in close-up, in slow motion, like one of those crime scene shows on TV. I see the barrel of the gun. I see the bullet come spiraling out of it, heading right for Martin. I see it make contact. I see his head—

If I'm lucky, that's when I wake up screaming.

If I'm not lucky, I have to watch it happen. And then I see the gun turn on me. I hear an explosion, like a cannon being fired, and I see a bullet spiraling toward me this time, heading straight for the spot between my eyes.

I hear myself scream. I feel it hit me—it's burning hot. It sears through me. The next thing I know, I'm sitting up in bed, soaking wet with sweat, tears streaming down my face.

And my kid sister wants to give me a hard time about smoking a couple of joints?

Okay, so maybe Martin wasn't as accommodating as he usually was when I said I hoped he was going to deliver on the party favors that night. He'd been a real downer for a few weeks before that, turning into a real grouch whenever I suggested we have a little fun. He always had some excuse why he didn't want to—he had too much homework; he was in a hurry to get to his volunteer job with Doctors Without Borders, which all of a sudden seemed like the most important thing in the world; he was short on cash (which I knew was a crock—his dad always saw to it that he had walking-around money). It was like he was turning into a different person. I had to really work it to get him to deliver, and even then…God, I hate Kelly. I hate the way she thinks she has me all figured out. I especially hate it when she turns out to be right.

I pretty much kept at Martin for the whole three days before the party, until, for the first time ever, he exploded.

"Jeez," he said. "Are you ever going to just shut up about it?"

I was so surprised that all I could do was stare at him. I felt like I was going to burst into tears, but I refused to let that happen, not while I was sitting there in the cafeteria, not when so many heads had turned to look at us.

"Fine," he snarled. He jumped up, making even more noise as his chair scraped against the floor, and stormed out of the cafeteria.

I glanced at Clark, who wasn't the least bit sympathetic. Clark had gone all straitlaced after his accident, at least where weed was concerned. Right after it happened, he said his parents had been all over him with: *Do you want to end up like your brother Scott?* I couldn't believe it. Clark and Martin were practically my best friends. We used to party every weekend. Then, all of a sudden, they both went all serious on me.

But Martin produced at the party. And, with a little coaxing, he finally joined the fun. He kept looking at me too, but not the way he used to. It was like he was trying to read my soul, and, I swear to God, he was on the edge of telling me something. He would have too, when he and Clark dropped me off at my house. I know he would have. I'm not the completely self-centered bitch my sister makes me out to be. I can read people. I read Martin that night. I knew exactly what was going to happen.

Clark was going to pull over in front of my house, just like always.

Martin was going to get out and open my door for me, just like always.

Only this time he was going to go with me up the walk.

This time he was going to tell me what had been on his mind all night.

This time, he was going to kiss me.

I just knew it.

The day went from merely sucking to sucking the big one.

My best friend, Gina, called—it was the first time I'd talked to her since it happened.

"You still mad at me?" I asked. She'd been angry when she found out that I'd been invited to Thomas's party but she hadn't. She'd asked me to ask Thomas to invite her too. I told her I would, but I didn't. Thomas wasn't hot on Gina, and I didn't want to get myself crossed off his invitation list because I'd badgered him about her.

"Of course not," she said, as if she hadn't shrieked at me and accused me of not trying hard enough to get her onto the guest list. "Did you hear the news?"

"What news?"

"I heard Martin's parents talked to Clark's parents about having a joint funeral. It makes sense, right? Clark and Martin were best friends. They have tons of friends in common. They went to the same school, which means a lot of the same teachers are going to want to be there. Also, if you ask me, they would have wanted to be together, don't you think?"

"I guess." The truth was, I hadn't thought about funerals. Maybe I didn't want to think about them.

"Clark's parents said no," Gina said.

"What? Why would they do that?"

"I heard from Sara, who got it directly from Anna"— Anna is one of Martin's sisters. She goes to my school too—"that they weren't very nice about it either. You know how they can be, especially Clark's mom."

I knew all right. She was stuck up. She'd grown up rich, she'd married rich, and she thought she was better than everyone else because of it. She especially thought she was better than Mr. and Mrs. Genovese—one who had never finished school, and the other who had come over from the Azores without a word of English and had worked nights as an office cleaner even after she married Mr. Genovese, using her paycheck to run the household while every penny he made went into building his business. Mrs. Carson had never liked that her precious

Clark's best friend was the son of two such unworthy people.

So there were two funerals, both on the same day: Clark's at the United Church two blocks from Clark's house; Martin's in the Catholic Church downtown in the old neighborhood where the Genoveses used to live before they made it big. Martin's funeral was at 11:00 AM, Clark's at 1:00 PM, which meant that the people at Martin's funeral who knew both Martin and Clark kept glancing at their watches, calculating how much time they would need to get uptown and find parking in order to be on time for Clark's service. Some kids—insensitive jerks, if you ask me—slipped out of the church before Martin's body even came down the aisle. But not me. And not Gina. I made her stay with me to the end. We grabbed a taxi. We arrived at Clark's funeral a little late, mostly because of traffic, but I didn't think anyone would notice, and we didn't mean any disrespect.

After the service, I approached the Carsons. I wanted Gina to come with me, but she said no, she wasn't good at talking to people who had just lost a loved one. Some friend! It wasn't as if I'd had tons of practice. My stomach churned as I wormed my way through the crowd that had gathered around Mr. and Mrs. Carson. They were watching Clark's casket being loaded into the hearse.

"Tegan," Mrs. Carson said, managing to look down at me even though we were the same height. "So glad you could make it for at least part of the service." There was no warmth in her voice, only disapproval.

Mr. Carson turned when he heard my name. His eyes were hard and as cold as his wife's voice.

"I'm sorry," I stammered. "I didn't mean to be late. It's just that—"

They turned their backs on me. I was so stunned that tears started to roll down my cheeks.

Someone grabbed my elbow and pulled me away. It was Gina.

"I don't think they're mad because we were late," she said in a soft voice that no one else could hear. "I think it's just, you know, the circumstances."

"What do you mean?"

"You know." Gina squirmed, as if she all of a sudden had to pee.

"No, I don't," I said.

"Because you were there."

"So?"

"Because you told the cops you didn't see anything."

"I didn't see anything."

"I know," Gina said quickly. "I just think they're having trouble understanding that." She hesitated a moment. "A lot of people are, Teeg."

A lot of people? I felt like crying all over again.

Gina put her arm around me. It made me feel good, like at least one person believed me. Then she said, "Are you sure you didn't see anything?"

"Am I *sure*?"

"What I mean is—"

"Am I *sure*?" What was the matter with her? "Don't you think that if I'd seen anything—anything at all—I would have told the cops?"

"I'm just saying—"

"It happened so fast. It was over before I knew what was going on."

Gina was looking around nervously, and no wonder. People were staring at me. I saw Mr. and Mrs. Carson through the crowd. They were looking at me too.

"I didn't see anything," I hissed. Then I got out of there.

ELEVEN

Kelly

INT.—TYRELL LIVING ROOM—DAY

KELLY is sitting in the living room, staring into space. She is wearing a black skirt, a black sweater and black tights. In her hand is a prayer card, a memento from Martin's funeral. She looks up listlessly when she hears the front door open. TEGAN and GINA appear, both dressed as if for a funeral. TEGAN looks like she's been crying. GINA is trying to comfort her.

> GINA
> (as if by rote)
> Just ignore them. They're upset. You really can't blame them.

                    KELLY
Who's upset?

                    TEGAN
            (ignoring her sister)
They hate me.

                    KELLY
Who hates you?

                    GINA
They don't hate you. They just lost their son. And
after what happened to Scott...

                    KELLY
You're crying because of the *Carsons*? They're total
snobs. And Clark was such an ass—

TEGAN swings around and slaps Kelly hard on the face.
The sound echoes in the suddenly silent room. GINA
stares at her friend in disbelief. She looks uncomfortable.

                    GINA
Maybe I should go.

                        80

                              TEGAN
No, don't.

KELLY has a hand to her cheek where Tegan slapped her.
She turns slowly and leaves the room.

CUT TO:

INT.—KELLY'S BEDROOM—DAY

KELLY enters her room. She slowly and deliberately closes
the door behind herself and crosses to her dresser. She
stares into the mirror at the red hand mark on her cheek.

                              KELLY
            (to the camera as she looks into the mirror)
He *was* an asshole. Clark Carson was an asshole, and
if you ask me, his parents are to blame. He thought
he was better than anyone else. He gave people a hard
time all the time.

DISSOLVE TO FLASHBACK:

INT.—HIGH SCHOOL HALLWAY—DAY

A short, thin boy is carrying a stack of textbooks down
the hall. Suddenly he topples forward. The books fly
out of his hands in slow motion. In slow motion—

and in silence—they cascade to the floor. So does the boy. The camera pulls back to reveal a foot sticking out into the hall. The camera pans slowly up the foot, the leg, the torso, to a silently laughing face. It is CLARK's face. The sound kicks in. CLARK is laughing. Everyone in the hall is laughing—except the boy on the floor, and KELLY, who watches in disgust from down the hall.

CUT BACK TO:
INT.—KELLY'S BEDROOM—DAY
KELLY is facing the camera.

> KELLY
> He was one of those guys who got a real kick out of making other people miserable.

DISSOLVE TO FLASHBACK:
INT.—HIGH SCHOOL CAFETERIA—DAY
A chubby girl is sitting alone at a small table at the back of the cafeteria. On the table in front of her is a plastic container. Inside are carrot and celery sticks. The girl is munching slowly on these as she leafs through a fashion magazine. Around her, the cafeteria bustles with the usual lunchtime comings and goings. The background noise is a cacophony of talking and laughing.

A PIZZA DELIVERY GUY appears, carrying three large pizza boxes. He walks toward the rear of the cafeteria. Kids stop what they are doing to look at him. He keeps walking. He doesn't stop until he gets to the chubby girl's table.

> PIZZA DELIVERY GUY
>
> Gail Worthington?

> GAIL
> (confused)
>
> Yes?

The PIZZA DELIVERY GUY sets the pizza boxes on Gail's table.

> GAIL (CONT'D)
>
> I didn't order these.

The PIZZA DELIVERY GUY takes a pitch pipe out of his pocket and blows into it. He starts to sing.

> PIZZA DELIVERY GUY
>
> Gail, we know you're trying hard
> To shed unwanted weight,

To take off all that fat and lard
So you can get a date.

GAIL glances around. Everyone is staring at her. She slouches in her chair and looks as if she wishes she could melt away.

> PIZZA DELIVERY GUY (CONT'D)
> You've given up the things you love
> Like ice cream, cake and pie.
> You've traded them for veggie sticks.
> It's so sad, we could cry.
>
> But we've seen your sacrifice.
> And the discipline you've found.
> So here's our gift to you, dear Gail,
> For losing *one whole pound*.

The cafeteria explodes in laughter. GAIL is mortified. She stares at the pizza boxes. Tears well up in her eyes. The PIZZA DELIVERY GUY retreats. We see a hand reach out with money. The camera pans slowly up the arm to the shoulder, then the face. CLARK laughs as he presses the money into the pizza delivery guy's hand.

CUT BACK TO:

INT. —KELLY'S BEDROOM—DAY

KELLY

Yeah, a real jerk. He was the kind of guy who could turn *you* into a jerk. You know, into one of those people who laughs at other people's misfortune. Well, at *his* misfortune. Not that he didn't deserve it.

Take the time I had that dentist's appointment. I'd just finished and I stepped out onto the street. It was like a neutron bomb had gone off or something. There was nothing moving out there except for me. Then I saw a car slide by.

DISSOLVE TO FLASHBACK:

EXT. —CITY STREET—DAY

A black Lexus van slides past KELLY, who is standing on the sidewalk. The van stops and then begins to back into a parking space. But before it can get there, a second car, also a Lexus, zips into the space headfirst. The driver of the second car gets out, grinning. It's CLARK. He spots Kelly and waves to her. KELLY groans and rolls her eyes. She watches the first car pull into another parking spot

85

farther down the street. The driver gets out. He opens the rear hatch of the van and then walks away from the car. KELLY frowns. What is he doing? Meanwhile, CLARK, oblivious of the other driver, approaches Kelly.

> CLARK
> If it isn't the other Tyrell twin.

> KELLY
> (annoyed)
> We're not twins.

KELLY looks over Clark's shoulder. The DRIVER of the other car is fast approaching. He's not an especially big man. In fact, he's rather slight, although he is easily as tall as Clark. He is dressed head-to-toe in black—black jeans, black T-shirt, long black overcoat, black boots—and has shoulder-length black hair. He is dark-skinned and is wearing mirrored sunglasses. A nasty scar runs diagonally from the middle of his chin to the middle of his right cheek.

> CLARK
> (to Kelly)
> The one with no sense of humor. The one...Hey!

The OTHER DRIVER has grabbed Clark roughly by the arm. He spins Clark around.

OTHER DRIVER

That was my space. You didn't see me ready to back in?

CLARK

(annoyed now that he sees who is daring to touch him)
No, I didn't. Now if you don't mind—

OTHER DRIVER

I mind. That was my spot. I was there first.

CLARK jerks his arm free.

CLARK

Well, it's mine now.

He turns from the other driver to Kelly and is about to say something when a shrill sound rips through the air. The OTHER DRIVER has whistled. In response, two dogs bound from the back of his van and race to his side. KELLY takes an automatic step backward when she recognizes the dogs as pit bulls. They are not leashed. The OTHER DRIVER points at Clark and snaps his fingers.

The dogs dart in front of Clark, growling. They look nasty.

> CLARK
> (trying to hide his fear)
> Hey, man. Call off your dogs.

> OTHER DRIVER
> You owe me an apology.

> CLARK
> Jeez, it's a parking space on a public street. You found another space. What's the big deal?

The OTHER DRIVER snaps his fingers again. This time the dogs start jumping at CLARK, who can no longer hide his fear.

> CLARK (CONT'D)
> Jesus!

CLARK fumbles in his jacket pocket for his cell phone. He pulls it out without once taking his eyes off the dogs, which are still growling.

CLARK (CONT'D)
Call them off or I'll—

The OTHER DRIVER says "Hand," and one of the dogs
snaps at Clark's hand. He drops his cell phone in terror as
his hand flies up out of reach of the dog.

OTHER DRIVER
Or you'll what?

KELLY moves back a few more steps. No way does she
want to get involved in this. She doesn't want the other
driver to know she even knows Clark.

OTHER DRIVER (CONT'D)
There are other commands I can give them. Ones you
won't like.

CLARK says nothing.

OTHER DRIVER (CONT'D)
Like att—

The OTHER DRIVER breaks off as a wet patch appears
on the front of Clark's pants. He has wet himself.

KELLY stares at him. The OTHER DRIVER grins.

> OTHER DRIVER (CONT'D)
> About that apology…

> CLARK
> I'm sorry, okay? Jesus! I'm sorry. I'm sorry.

The OTHER DRIVER snaps his fingers and the dogs fall instantly silent.

> OTHER DRIVER
> Don't let it happen again.

He says "Heel," and the two dogs fall in on either side of him. KELLY watches him walk away. CLARK stands motionless for a full minute. Finally, in a small, strangled-sounding voice, he speaks.

> CLARK
> Is he gone?

KELLY nods. CLARK turns around. His whole body seems to sag with relief. He turns back to KELLY, who is staring at his crotch. CLARK's face turns red. He takes off his jacket and holds it in front of himself.

> CLARK (CONT'D)
> If you tell anyone about this...

KELLY just stares at him. She watches him walk to his own car, then pause, then walk up to the other driver's car, where he stands, studying it. Finally he gets back into his own car. A moment later it squeals away from the curb, and KELLY starts to laugh.

> KELLY
> (to herself)
> Where's an audience when you need one?

CUT BACK TO:
INT.—KELLY'S BEDROOM—DAY

> KELLY
> (to the camera)
> The thing is, I didn't tell. I wanted to. But I kept seeing the look on his face—not Clark's face, the other guy's. He was mean. And those dogs? They were weapons,

and the guy knew it. I don't know. After everything Clark did, there are a lot of kids who would have pissed themselves laughing over that story. But I just couldn't do it. I couldn't tell. Not even Tegan. Clark didn't look at me for weeks. After that, well, when he did see me, he had a kind of scared look to him all over again, like he was afraid I was going to say something. Like he was afraid everyone was going to laugh at him like they did at Gail or at that kid in the hall he tripped.

(sighing)

I guess I didn't tell anyone because of what my mom calls the good-guy rule. In a movie, the bad guy can do pretty much whatever heinous thing he wants—he can rape and kill and mutilate. But the good guy—he's not supposed to do stuff like that because if he did, well, what would make him any different from the bad guy? Another way my mother puts it: "There are enough jerks in the world, Kelly. You don't need to add to that number." But, boy, you have no idea how close I came to spilling the beans.

TWELVE
Tegan

I hate to admit it—I hate to admit anything that will make Kelly gloat—but Clark really could be a jerk. According to Martin, it wasn't always that way. Martin knew Clark from when they were in elementary school. The way Martin told it, Clark was so shy back then that he never looked anyone in the eye when he talked to them—that is, when he was forced to talk. He hardly ever initiated a conversation. And because he was so shy, he was always on the sidelines. When teams were picked, he was always the last one chosen.

"I guess I felt sorry for him," Martin told me one time. "I just kept going up to him and talking to him and asking him to sit with me at lunch, stuff like that. And after a while, he kind of opened up."

Kind of.

Clark's brother Scott, who is three years older than Clark, was the golden boy of the family. He was good-looking (so was Clark, but back then, according to Martin, he never would have believed it). He was smart—top grades all the way through school. He was athletic—captain of the football team, star soccer player, high-scorer in his hockey league. He was a charmer—teachers liked him, adults liked him, kids his own age liked him. He could make anyone laugh. He was hugely popular.

Clark, on the other hand, had more of a struggle with school. He never actually failed anything. He was in solid B territory all the way through and, according to Martin, worked hard for those grades. But it wasn't good enough for his teachers, who always compared him to Scott. It wasn't good enough for his parents either. They demanded straight As. Clark wasn't as good at sports as Scott had been. Sure, he made the team. But he wasn't always first-string.

And then there was the stuttering.

When he was little, Clark had a terrible stutter. That turned out to be the reason he was so quiet and shy.

The more nervous he was, the worse the stutter became. And kids, being kids, naturally made fun of him.

His parents, again, according to Martin, regarded him as damaged goods because of the stutter. His father always finished sentences for him. He told Clark he'd never make good if he didn't learn to talk like a man. His mother was more supportive, Martin said, but she had a pained expression on her face whenever Clark spoke in front of her friends. Her solution was to send him for intensive speech therapy. He went three times a week for years. The therapist tried all kinds of ways to get him to stop stuttering.

"I was at his house one time after school," Martin said. "His dad burst into his room without even knocking. He had a piece of paper in his hand. It was a bill from the speech therapist. He ripped into Clark because he was spending all that money and the stuttering wasn't getting any better. The thing is, it *was* better. Whenever it was just Clark and me, he hardly ever stuttered. But around his dad it was awful."

But by the time Clark started junior high, he'd got his stutter under control. He hardly ever stuttered. But it didn't seem to make any difference to his dad. Once Clark stopped stuttering, his dad got after him for his grades. Then for the fact that he wasn't as good an athlete as Scott.

His dad was always knocking him. If you ask me, that's why Clark persecuted other kids—to feel better about himself. So, yes, he could be a jerk. But he didn't start off that way. If he'd had different parents—if he'd had a different dad—he probably would have been a different Clark.

And then Scott had his accident.

Perfect popular Scott went out and got wasted one night and then climbed into his expensive car, revved it up and failed to navigate a bend in the road. Result: he literally wrapped his car around a utility pole. He was in the hospital for months. He severed his spinal cord and ended up in a wheelchair. He suffered brain damage. He wasn't charming anymore. He wasn't funny. He wasn't athletic. He wasn't even handsome. He was just poor Scott who needed round-the-clock care and whose mother spent a fortune on physiotherapy for him the way she'd spent a fortune on speech therapy for Clark. Except that Scott was never going to get better.

Overnight, Clark became his father's son, the one who would carry on the family name and inherit the family fortune. His father gave him everything he wanted. He called him "my son," making it sound like he only had one. Clark wasn't fooled. He knew what his dad was up to. He'd never forgiven his father for the way he had treated Clark before Scott's accident. But he didn't give his dad grief. No way. Instead, he milked it for everything he could get. And he kept right on trying to feel good about himself by proving time after time that he wasn't as pathetic as a lot of other kids.

He could be such a jerk that sometimes I wanted to tell him exactly what I thought of him: You're an asshole, Clark. You're a bully, Clark. You, of all people, should know better than to make fun of others. You should know better than to do stupid stuff like that.

Except there was one other thing about Clark: he never forgot and he never forgave. If you crossed him, he crossed you off his list, forever.

And, well, he just wasn't a big enough jerk for me to want that to happen. Clark always had money. He always knew where there was a party. If there was nothing happening, he could fix that. And, of course, where Clark was, Martin was too. If I'd ever told Clark exactly what I thought of him, I probably would never have seen Martin again. Besides, Clark never gave me a hard time. Well, hardly ever.

And Martin didn't seem bothered by him, so why should I be?

Martin.

He was so sweet. And fun. Especially when he was mellow. Boy, could he ever make me laugh. He was cute too. And smart. And kind. I liked that about him. I was sure it was going to happen between us.

And then Gina told me that Anna had told her that Martin had a thing for my sister—for straight-ahead, never-party Kelly. What on earth did he see in her? I didn't believe it. Except that he didn't want to party anymore, and he started to worry about getting busted for drugs because that would be the end of his dream of medical school. Like doctors aren't supposed to have any fun.

No, I'm sure it wouldn't have happened the way Gina said. I mean, at first he didn't want to score so we could have a great time after midterms. But I turned that one around, didn't I? We had a blast. And I saw the way he looked at me that night. I was there. Anna wasn't. Neither was Gina. Or Kelly. No, if things hadn't happened the way they did that night, Martin and I could have ended up together. I know we would've.

But they did happen.

And now they were both gone—Clark and Martin. And not only did I have to live with that—with what I'd seen, with what people thought I'd seen, with everything that people were saying—but I had to face everyone too. Sooner or later, I had to go back to school. Alone. Without Martin and Clark.

I didn't know how I was going to manage it.

THIRTEEN

Kelly

INT.—TYRELL KITCHEN—DAY

MRS. TYRELL is standing at the counter, drinking the last of a cup of coffee. She is wearing a business suit. KELLY is sitting at the table, eating a piece of toast. TEGAN is in the doorway to the kitchen, a scowl on her face.

MRS. TYRELL

It will be good for you. Carla says that Bradley says the best thing you can do is get back into your regular routine.

KELLY

(to the camera)

Carla is my mother's best friend. Her husband, Bradley, is a psychiatrist.

MRS. TYRELL

Besides, you don't want to lose your school year, do you?

TEGAN

I just lost two of my best friends. What do I care about the school year?

MRS. TYRELL

You can't give up. We all face a lot of hurt in life, Tegan. We're all called upon to be strong. Clark and Martin wouldn't have wanted your life to stop just because theirs did. I know they wouldn't. Kelly will walk with you.

KELLY

No, she won't.

MRS. TYRELL

Tegan is your sister. She's been through something you can't even begin to imagine. You'll walk with her and you'll look out for her.

KELLY

Why doesn't she walk to school with Gina? Gina's her best friend.

MRS. TYRELL looks inquiringly at TEGAN, who shakes her head miserably.

MRS. TYRELL
She wants you to walk with her.

KELLY looks at her mother as if her mother has taken complete leave of her senses.

KELLY
No, she doesn't.

KELLY glances at Tegan.

KELLY (CONT'D)
Do you, Teeg?

TEGAN
(pale-faced)
Actually, Kel, I kinda do.

MRS. TYRELL

Then it's settled.

KELLY

(to the camera)

My plan: wait until Mom leaves for work and then take off by myself. Jeez, who does she think she is? Tegan, I mean. She's spent the last couple of days telling me to mind my own business. And now she wants my help? Fat chance!

MRS. TYRELL remains where she is, arms crossed over her chest.

MRS. TYRELL

Well? Go and get your things, Tegan.

TEGAN shoots an annoyed look at her mother.

KELLY

(to camera)

Well, what do you know? Big sister is thinking the same thing I am—only in her case it's wait until Mom leaves and then go back up to her room.

TEGAN leaves the kitchen. Footsteps are heard going up the stairs and then, a moment later, coming back down again. TEGAN reappears, backpack slung over one shoulder. MRS. TYRELL pushes herself away from the counter and walks the girls to the door.

CUT TO:
INT.—HIGH SCHOOL HALLWAY—DAY
KELLY stands impatiently beside a locker as TEGAN works the combination to open the lock.

> KELLY
> (impatiently)
> I have to go, Teeg. I have to get to *my* locker.

> TEGAN
> Just a sec. I'll go with you. I promise.

> KELLY
> I don't need you to go with me.

KELLY pushes away from the locker she's been leaning on. TEGAN grabs her arm.

TEGAN

Please, Kel? Just for today.

KELLY

What's the matter with you? Where's Gina?

TEGAN

(angry)

Why do you keep asking me about Gina? What does she have to do with anything?

KELLY

Trouble in best-friend paradise?

TEGAN

Please, Kel? People keep looking at me. They're looking at me now. I don't like it.

KELLY glances around the crowded corridor. Sure enough, kids are staring at Tegan. Some of them are talking while their eyes are glued to her.

KELLY

They're just curious. I bet Clark and Martin are the

first kids in the whole history of this school who have
ever been shot.

TEGAN

That's not it. That's not why they're staring at me.

KELLY

What do you mean?

Before TEGAN can answer, she sees a girl approaching her.
She is petite and slender, with long dark hair and piercing
brown eyes. She is ANNA GENOVESE, Martin's sister.

TEGAN

Oh my god! It's Anna. What am I going to say to her?

ANNA walks straight up to Tegan. She thrusts out her
hands and slams Tegan against the wall of lockers.

ANNA

Bitch! Lying bitch!

The hallway filled with students falls silent, as if someone
has thrown a switch, shutting off the audio.

ANNA (CONT'D)

How dare you tell the cops my brother was a drug dealer!

TEGAN looks at her in dismay.

TEGAN

I never said that.

ANNA

First you lie about Martin. Now you're lying to me.

ANNA looks around at the kids in the hall as if making sure that everyone is listening.

TEGAN

I never said anything to the cops about drugs. I never said Martin was a drug dealer.

ANNA

Then how come the cops came to my house and asked my mom and dad and my sisters what we knew about Martin using drugs? You should have seen the look on my mother's face. It was like that cop had reached right into her chest and ripped her heart out.

TEGAN

I didn't say anything to the cops about Martin doing drugs.

KELLY peers intently at her sister.

ANNA

Stop lying.

TEGAN

I'm not lying.

ANNA

The cops said Martin smoked up the night he died.

TEGAN

They probably got that from the autopsy report.

ANNA

They said a lot of people at the party smoked up and that Martin was the one who supplied the weed. My mother started to cry when they said that. She's afraid he was some kind of criminal.

TEGAN

They must have asked someone at the party. They
didn't say anything to me about that.

KELLY
(to the camera)
She's hiding something. I know that look on her face.

ANNA

The cops asked us if we knew where Martin got the
drugs he brought to the party. They asked about
everyone Martin had ever talked to, everyone he
had ever called—they said they were going to look
through his cell-phone records, and they took his
computer. My dad asked them why they were doing
all that. You know what they said? Do you?
(glaring at Tegan)
They said that it's possible Martin's death was drug-
related. You know what that means, right? It means
they think it's Martin's fault he got killed. They think
it's because he was a drug dealer.

TEGAN
(clearly shaken)
It wasn't me. I didn't say anything like that.

ANNA glances at her audience again, making sure that everyone is paying close attention.

> ANNA
>
> My dad called Clark's dad to ask him if the cops were asking the same kind of questions about Clark. Mr. Carson said of course not. He said that Clark hadn't done any drugs that night—he said the autopsy report proves it. He said Clark never did any drugs, like Clark was an angel and Martin was the devil. Martin was ten thousand times nicer than Clark. He didn't make fun of people the way Clark did or push them around or key their cars for no reason.

> TEGAN
>
> Anna, I—

> ANNA
>
> Mr. Carson said that he'd hired an investigator of his own to ask some questions. He said the investigator talked to you and that you knew that Martin had a drug connection.

KELLY stares at her sister.

KELLY
(to the camera)
I knew it. I knew she was hiding something.

TEGAN
I didn't say that.

ANNA
He also said that that's why you weren't cooperating with the police—because you knew all about it and you must have seen the guy who did it, but you're too much of a coward to tell the truth.

TEGAN
That's not true. None of it's true.

ANNA
He said that if it wasn't for Martin and his drug buddies, Clark would still be alive. The Carsons are blaming Martin too. Everyone's blaming Martin.

TEGAN
I'm sure that's not true. I'm sure no one blames Martin.

SHE SAID / SHE SAW

ANNA

Really? Then how come the cops are at school today?
How come they want to talk to everyone who knew
Martin?

ANNA's hands are curled into fists. Her face is twisted.
She spits at Tegan, hitting her square in the face.

ANNA (CONT'D)
I wish Martin never knew you. I hope you rot in Hell.

She turns and strides down the hall, the heels of her
shoes *click-clicking*, past a hallway full of kids who are
standing so still it looks like they're painted on a back-
drop. TEGAN fumbles in her pockets but comes up
empty. She wipes the spit off her face with the sleeve of
her sweater. Then she peels the sweater off and stuffs it in
her locker. She slams the locker shut and runs down the
hall. KELLY watches her push open the door to the girls'
bathroom. She looks up and down the hallway at all the
faces that are still turned in Tegan's direction.

FOURTEEN

Tegan

Ms. Richards, the principal, made an announcement over the PA system during home form. She said that the police were going to be at the school all day and that they wanted to talk to anyone who knew Clark and Martin. She said that no one *had* to talk to them, but that she was sure everyone wanted to do what they could to help the police catch whoever had taken two such young and promising lives. Anyone who wanted to could ask for a pass to go down to the office to speak to the police. She also said that the police had some kids they wanted to talk to. Again, she stressed that no one was under any obligation to talk to them and that anyone who decided they had something to say was entitled to have a parent or other adult with them if they wanted. If someone wanted a parent with them but it wasn't possible to do that today, she said we could give the police our names and phone numbers and they would arrange an appointment.

In my home form, Sara Renard asked for a pass to go to the office. She was on the student council with Clark. I don't know what she wanted to tell the cops, but she gave me a sharp look as she walked by my desk, as if to let me know that she was going to do something that I hadn't—she was going to tell the police everything she knew. At least a couple of kids in every one of my classes that morning asked for passes too. A lot of people knew Clark and Martin. I wondered how many went down to the office. I wondered what they were saying.

Then, just before lunch, Mrs. Esterhazy, the vice-principal, showed up at the door of my history class and spoke to Mr. Vincent, my history teacher. I saw Detective Zorbas standing beside her. Mr. Vincent called out Tim Maxwell's name and beckoned him to the front of the room. He stepped out into the hall, and Mrs. Esterhazy closed the door behind him. Zorbas said something to Tim. I felt like I was going to faint. This was getting worse and worse.

I jumped on Tim Maxwell the minute he stepped out into the schoolyard.

"What did you tell the cops?"

"Jeez, you startled me, Tegan." He offered me a nervous smile.

"You went to the office to talk to the cops. What did you tell them?"

The smile vanished from his face. "That's none of your business."

"What do you mean it's none of my business? I was with them when it happened. I saw them get killed. Do you have any idea what that's like? There was blood everywhere. Clark's blood. Martin's blood. They were shot in the head. Both of them. You have any idea what that looks like?"

"Shit, calm down." Tim glanced around the schoolyard, probably wishing there was someone else nearby, preferably a friend of his, to bail him out.

"You went down to the office. You had something you wanted to talk to the cops about. If anyone has a right to know what you told them, it's me."

He stared at me and then looked away, like he was trying to decide what to do—tell me or make a run for it.

"Okay, first of all," he said, "I didn't go down to the office. I was called there. And Richards sent Esterhazy up to get me and escort me down. I didn't have any choice." He sounded mad. "Someone must have ratted me out." He stared directly at me.

"It wasn't me."

"Well, it was someone, because before they started, they went through all my rights and asked me if I wanted to call my parents, you know, because I had a right to have them there if I wanted to. I asked them what was going on. You can't make up your mind what to do unless you know what's going on. They said it was about Martin and Clark getting shot. They said they knew I'd bought drugs from Martin. They *knew*, and they weren't bluffing either. They asked me again if I wanted someone with me while I talked to them. Come on, like I was going to have them call my dad and get him to leave work to listen to me getting grilled by the cops over some weed I got from Martin. You have any idea what my old man would do if he knew about that? And my mom—" He shook his head. "She'd tell my dad even if I begged her not to. So, no, the last thing I wanted was to have one of my parents there. They made me sign a paper that I had refused to have someone present. Cops, they're always covering their asses."

"What did you tell them?"

"They told me if I cooperated, they wouldn't charge me with anything."

"Charge you? What could they charge you with?"

"They knew I bought drugs from him. If I bought drugs from him, they could get me on possession."

"They can't do that unless they actually find weed on you."

"They *knew*, Tegan. They knew about my birthday. Someone told them. They had a witness."

"What exactly did you tell them, Tim?"

"I didn't *tell* them. I confirmed what they already knew—I didn't have any choice."

"Confirmed what exactly?"

"Like I said, that when I wanted some weed to celebrate, I bought it from Martin."

"Did you say it like that—that you bought drugs from him? Or did you say something else?"

"Like what?"

Like what? I started to feel sick. "How about that Martin wasn't a drug dealer?"

"He sold them to me, Tegan. So technically—"

"Don't give me technically. Did you tell them you wanted to buy weed because after a whole year of trying, you finally got that slut Miranda Taschereau to go out with you, but that she only agreed because you promised her you had some good weed—which you didn't? That you had to beg Martin to give you a few joints, which he didn't want to do, and that you finally offered to do what you should have done in the first place, which is to pay him for the stuff? You didn't go to him because he was a drug dealer. You went to him because you knew he had some weed and you wanted to get your cheap little hands on some of it so you could score with Miranda, who, by the way, probably had an STD."

His face was red. He stared stonily at me.

"You didn't tell them *that*, did you?" I was practically screaming at him. I grabbed his arm.

"They sent for me. I didn't volunteer to go down there. They told me they knew I'd bought weed from him. They said they wouldn't make things hard for me if I played straight with them. They basically just wanted me to confirm something they already knew, which is that I had got drugs from him. Then they wanted to know if I knew where he got the drugs, who he got them from, which I didn't. I told them I didn't ask and that, even if I had, he probably wouldn't have told me."

"You made him sound like a dealer."

"Look, he had the weed. A lot of people knew he had it. I didn't make him buy it. I had nothing to do with it. If he had a drug problem—"

"He didn't have a drug problem any more than you have a drug problem!"

"Well, he had some kind of problem because his drug connection shot him dead."

"What? Did the cops say that to you?"

"It's what they were getting at."

"Did they say it?"

"I can read between the lines, Tegan. Martin and Clark get shot. Martin gets it first, so obviously he was the target. Clark gets it because he was in the wrong place at the wrong time. You're still alive because whoever did it probably didn't see you there in the back seat on account of those tinted windows Clark had—"

"Martin wasn't a drug dealer."

"Those cops aren't stupid. They know what they're doing. They know all kinds of stuff."

"You're making things worse, Tim. You're dishonoring Martin. You're making him out to be something he wasn't. You're blaming him for what happened."

"*I'm* dishonoring him? You were there, Tegan. You saw what happened. You just told me so yourself. If you weren't so chickenshit, you would help the cops catch whoever did it."

"I didn't see anything."

"Right. You're right there in the back seat, but you didn't see a thing. You know what it was about, Tegan. That's why you're refusing to tell them anything."

Refusing?

"Those guys who are into drugs, you don't want to fool with them. You rat one of those guys out and you're dead. And you have the balls to tell me that *I'm* dishonoring Martin?"

He jerked his arm free.

"Besides, I'm not the only person they talked to," he said. "Steve talked to them too."

"Steve? He gave Steve one joint. One."

"Try telling the cops that. Those guys are hard-asses. Drugs are drugs. And the only person to blame for Martin getting into them is Martin himself."

Did u c it?

It was Gina, texting me. Asking me the same thing she'd asked at the funeral. At first I was going to ignore her message. But I didn't want to have to go through tomorrow the same way I'd gone through today, mostly alone except for lunchtime, when my bitchy sister deigned to eat with me. I knew that she only did it because she didn't want Mom to yell at her. I wanted to be with someone who wanted to be with me. I wanted a friend. I wanted Gina, even if that meant I had to tell her a hundred times what I'd already told her the day of the funeral. So:

C what? I texted back.

The answer I got wasn't the one I expected.

The site.

What site?

My cell phone rang.

"The site someone put up," Gina said breathlessly. "About you. About what happened."

"What site?" I asked as I launched myself across the room in the direction of my computer. She gave me the URL, and I typed it in. The next thing I knew, I was staring at a photo of myself and, across my forehead, *What Tegan Saw*. I scanned the text and posts underneath. None of them were signed with real names, but they all said more or less the same thing—that I had seen Clark and Martin get shot but that I was refusing to cooperate with the police because I was afraid that the gang that had shot them would come after me and kill me.

"It's gone viral," Gina said. "I got a text from Sara. She got it from Britney, who got it from Dawn, who says she doesn't even know who sent it to her. The whole school has seen it."

It turned out that it had gone beyond that.

After I'd finished talking to Gina, the doorbell rang. I wanted to ignore it, but what if it was Mom? She often rang the bell when she got home late with her hands full of groceries or dry cleaning or work she had to get finished before the next day. When I opened the front door, I was almost blinded by a bright light—from a video camera.

"What do you think about the What Tegan Saw website?" a man asked me.

I held my hand up in front of my face to block the light.

"Whoever put it up doesn't know what they're talking about," I said.

"But you did see Clark Carson and Martin Genovese get shot, didn't you?" the man said.

"Yes. I mean, I saw what happened to them, but I didn't—"

"The police say the shots came from the driver's side. Is that right?"

"Yes, but—"

"Are you afraid that you're going to be next? Is that why you're refusing to cooperate with the police?"

"No, I—"

"You're not afraid that the killer will come after you, the only witness to the shooting?"

"I didn't see what happened."

"You just said you did."

"I saw them get shot, but that's all I saw. I didn't see who did it."

I slammed the door shut.

Did u c it?

Gina again, late that night.

C what?

News.

Then someone hammered on my bedroom door.

"Teeg, you up?"

It was Kelly.

"I'm on the phone!" I yelled through the closed door.

"Yeah, well, you're going to want to hear this. You were just on the news."

I sent a quick text to Gina—*Talk later*—and called at Kelly to come in.

"What about the news?" I asked her.

"You were on it. So was Mr. Carson. And the cops. They said Mr. Genovese wasn't available for comment."

"What did they say?"

"They showed a website about you. Then they showed a clip of you saying that you saw what happened to Martin and Clark. Then a clip of you saying that you didn't see what happened. Then they showed this cop saying that he hoped if you knew anything or saw anything, you would come forward so that they could catch whoever did it."

"What about Mr. Carson? What did he say?"

"Pretty much the same thing as the cops—that you should do the right thing and cooperate with the police. He said that he would forgive you and Martin for what happened if you would just tell the cops everything you know so that the person who killed Clark could be brought to justice."

"He said he'd *forgive* me and Martin?" As if we'd done something wrong. As if Clark was the only person who had been shot—or the only person who mattered. "I told that reporter that I didn't see who did it. I told everyone that. I feel like I could scream it from the rooftops and it wouldn't make any difference. No one believes me."

"I believe you," Kelly said.

"You do?"

I searched her face, but I couldn't tell if she was telling the truth or was just saying what she thought I wanted to hear.

She sank down onto my bed.

"I guess it must have been awful for you—"

"You *guess?*"

"You know what I mean, Teeg. And you know how people are. You're just going to have to tough it out. I don't know what else you can do."

I felt my stomach twisting up. I wanted to yell at her and everybody else. But she was right. People believed what they wanted to believe, and there was no way I could think of to make them change their minds.

Right after Kelly left my room, I called Gina.

"Are you okay?" she asked. She sounded worried.

"Yeah. I guess."

"You want me to swing by tomorrow morning and pick you up? You know, so you don't have to arrive at school alone?"

I wished I could have said, *Thanks, but I'll be fine.* But I wasn't at all sure I would be. It had been bad enough when Anna Genovese had come at me, screaming accusations so that everyone in the whole school could hear. But this website was something else. A whole lot more people besides Anna were talking about me, and they were all saying the same thing: that Martin was shot over drugs and that I was too afraid to come forward and tell the police who had done it.

There was no angry mob outside the school. Gina's sigh of relief was audible.

"Some of the comments on the site were pretty awful," she said. "And there were a lot more of them, Teeg, not all by kids from our school. I was a little afraid…"

We made our way up the front walk and into the school. Everything looked normal.

"You want me to come to your locker with you?" Gina said.

"No, I'll be all right. I'll see you in math, okay?"

FIFTEEN
Kelly

INT.—HIGH SCHOOL HALLWAY—DAY

KELLY is standing at her friend Lacey's locker when everyone around her falls silent. She looks way down the hall and sees TEGAN approach her locker. She notices that all the kids who, moments before, had been taking things out of their lockers or putting things inside are motionless now, but that none of them are looking at Tegan. She watches as TEGAN seems to notice too. TEGAN frowns, grabs her lock and starts dialing the combination. The silence continues as TEGAN takes out some textbooks and binders, closes the locker and leaves.

                    KELLY
What's going on?

LACEY bangs her locker shut. She is oblivious to what
has just happened.

                    LACEY
Huh?

                    KELLY
It was like everyone turned to stone when Tegan was
at her locker.

LACEY, baffled, merely shrugs.

CUT TO:

INT.—HIGH SCHOOL HALLWAY—DAY
A bell rings, classroom doors open up and down the hall,
and students pour out, moving quickly from one class to
the next. KELLY's face appears through the crowd. She is
looking for someone. She zeros in on her target and muscles
her way through a sea of kids who are going the opposite
direction. She reaches out to grab someone. TEGAN spins
around, a scared and startled look on her face.

KELLY

Are you okay?

TEGAN turns away, and KELLY follows her gaze. Down the hall, ANNA is saying something to Gina. GINA glances in Tegan's direction. ANNA says something else and then slips away into the crowd. GINA glances around and sees many eyes looking at her. She slowly makes her way toward Tegan and Kelly.

KELLY (CONT'D)

What was that about? What did Anna say to you?

GINA

You're invisible.

KELLY

What are you talking about? What's going on, Gina?

GINA

That's what she said to me. She said, "Tell your friend Tegan that she's invisible."

TEGAN moans. She sags a little. KELLY looks at her in dismay.

TEGAN

Nobody looked at me in home form. Nobody except Mrs. Persaud. No one has looked at me all morning. No one has talked to me either. It's like I don't exist.

GINA

Anna said it's going to stay that way until you do the right thing and tell the police everything you saw.

TEGAN
(close to tears)
I told her—I told everyone—I don't know anything.

KELLY
(to the camera)
This is like kindergarten all over again. God, I hate school.

GINA is clearly upset. She looks like she is bursting to say more, but something is holding her back. TEGAN notices.

TEGAN

What? Did she say something else?

GINA
(shaking her head)
It's just that...a lot of people are with her, Teeg.
I heard them talking.

KELLY
So? They're a bunch of idiots.

GINA looks only at Tegan.

GINA
Jamie is with her.

KELLY
Then Jamie's a moron.

GINA
(angry)
He is not!

TEGAN
She didn't mean it, Gina.

KELLY
I did so. Anyone who—

TEGAN reaches out and silences Kelly with a touch on her arm.

> TEGAN
> (softly)
> Gina and Jamie are, well, they're kind of getting together, you know?

TEGAN takes in the sad but hopeful look on Kelly's face.

> KELLY
> (to the camera)
> As if I didn't know. Jeez, Gina has had it bad for Jamie Dingwall practically since second grade. She's always staring moodily at him from across classrooms and down hallways. She keeps coming up with these lame excuses to talk to him. Okay, so maybe not so lame. Just last month, he actually started talking back. He even asked her out a couple of times, and Gina's over the moon. Still, if some guy *I* was interested in acted so childishly toward *my* best friend—

> GINA
> (to Tegan)
> He said there's no way a person could be sitting where

you were sitting and not see anything. Anna said that they've all decided—anyone who hangs with you is going to be invisible too.

KELLY

This just keeps getting more ridiculous. Anna's full of it, Gina.

TEGAN

There's no way Jamie's going to ignore you, Gina. He likes you. You told me that things were really clicking with you two.

GINA doesn't look so sure.

TEGAN (CONT'D)

Have you talked to him?

GINA shakes her head.

TEGAN (CONT'D)

Talk to him, Gina. You'll see.

KELLY

Yeah, talk to him, Gina. And if he still acts like a moron, dump him.

The bell rings. GINA hesitates and then scurries away. KELLY glances at Tegan.

KELLY

You okay?

TEGAN looks completely demoralized, but she manages a smile before they go their separate ways to their classes.

SIXTEEN

Tegan

Gina wasn't at her locker after school, even though we had agreed to meet there so we could walk home together. I waited around in case she'd got caught up in something at the end of her last class. Kids came to their lockers and left again. No one looked at me. No one spoke to me. I pretended I didn't see them either. But I did. I saw them and I wished none of this was happening. I wished Martin and Clark were still around. Kids would be looking at me then for sure. Clark and Martin were the ones everyone wanted to be with.

Gradually the hallway got quieter and quieter. Gina still didn't show up. I headed home.

I was standing on the porch unlocking the front door when she waved to me from the side of the house.

"Where were you?" I asked.

She didn't answer.

"Well, come on in," I said.

She didn't move. She stayed where she was and glanced nervously across the street. What was going on?

"Come *on*, Gina," I said. What did she want? An engraved invitation?

"You come here."

I pulled my key out of the lock and trudged down the porch steps toward her. When I got to the side of the house, she grabbed my arm and dragged me around to the backyard.

"What's the matter with you?" I said.

"Nothing."

"Where were you? You were supposed to wait for me."

Her eyes shifted to the ground.

"Sorry," she murmured. "Jamie was waiting for me in the hall after class. He walked me home."

"While I was standing at your locker pretending I didn't notice that everyone was making a point of not looking at me."

"I'm sorry, Teeg. You must have just missed me."

"Mr. Ashton was out sick. We had a spare. I spent last period in the library. I was at your locker before the last bell rang. I waited for half an hour."

Gina glanced at me for a nanosecond before returning her eyes to the apparently mesmerizing scene in my backyard.

"Oh," she said. "The thing is, Jamie and I left straight from class."

"So you didn't go to your locker at all?"

"No, I guess I didn't."

I looked at the bulging backpack she was wearing. There was no way she had dragged it to her afternoon classes. I felt like I was going to throw up. My best friend in the whole world was lying to me. She must have stashed her backpack somewhere else besides her locker—maybe in Jamie's locker. And the only reason I could think of for doing that was that she had wanted to avoid me.

"Did you talk to Jamie?" I asked.

"Yeah. But," she added quickly, "we didn't talk about you. I—it just didn't seem like the right time, you know?"

"Well, I guess that explains why you're hiding around here."

That got her attention. She looked up at me.

"What are you talking about?" she said. "Who says I'm hiding?"

"Well, aren't you? Isn't that why you waited for me around the side of the house and why you didn't come up on the porch when I asked you to? You didn't want Chris to see you, did you?" Chris Finney lived across the street. He was Jamie's best friend. "What's the matter? Afraid he'd tell Jamie you're fraternizing with the enemy?"

"No!" She even managed to look indignant.

"No?" I grabbed her hand. "Okay, so let's go sit on the front porch where we can get some sun." I started to pull her toward the side of the house.

"Hey!" She resisted. "Hey, let go!"

I dropped her arm as if it were on fire. Gina's shoulders slumped.

"I was going to talk to Jamie. Really, I was. But, well, it just wasn't the right time, Teeg. And he had his arm around me all the way home. And I—"

"You didn't want to kill the fairy tale. Yeah, I get it," I said.

"I'm going to talk to him."

"Right."

"I am!"

"Sure. And I guess you didn't want Chris to see you with me before you got the chance to have that talk with Jamie because you didn't want him to get the wrong idea, right?"

"Right." She sounded relieved.

Who did she think she was kidding?

"Let me know when you've found the guts to stick up for me."

I pushed past her and unlocked the back door.

"I said I was going to talk to him," she said, angry now, like she was the victim, like I was being unfair to her.

"If it was the other way around, if you were the one who was getting the silent treatment, I'd stick up for you," I said. "You know I would."

"And if I'd been in that car and had seen what you saw, I'd have told the cops everything the first time they asked me. I wouldn't be holding back because I was mad at one of the victims."

SEVENTEEN

Kelly

INT.—TYRELL KITCHEN—DAY

KELLY is standing at the kitchen sink, listening to voices outside.

GINA'S VOICE

And if I'd been in that car and had seen what you saw, I'd have told the cops everything the first time they asked me. I wouldn't be holding back because I was mad at one of the victims.

KELLY goes up on tiptoes so that she can bend over the sink and look out the window.

                    TEGAN'S VOICE
What are you talking about?

                    GINA'S VOICE
You know.

                    TEGAN'S VOICE
No, I don't.

                    GINA'S VOICE
You were mad at him.

KELLY frowns.

                    KELLY
                    (to the camera)
Mad at who?

                    TEGAN'S VOICE
Mad at who?

                    GINA'S VOICE
Mad at who? Mad at Martin, that's who. Because of
what I told you.

KELLY leans even closer to the window.

> TEGAN'S VOICE
> For your information, you're wrong. He didn't say a thing about her. In fact, he told me I was beautiful. *And* he had his arm around my waist.

> GINA'S VOICE
> He was probably trying to work up his nerve to tell you.

> TEGAN'S VOICE
> He was not!

> GINA'S VOICE
> He was worried. He told me so. But he said he had to do what he had to do—he said it was his heart.

> KELLY
> (still frowning, to the camera)
> His heart? Something was wrong with Martin's heart?

> TEGAN'S VOICE
> He *told* you? You said you overheard him talking to Clark. Now you're saying he told *you*?

GINA'S VOICE

He came up to me. He wanted some advice.

TEGAN'S VOICE

Martin wanted advice from *you*? About *me*?

GINA'S VOICE

He liked you, Tegan. He didn't want to hurt your feelings. He didn't want you to be mad at Kelly either.

TEGAN'S VOICE

You don't know what you're talking about! He wasn't interested in Kelly, not the way you're saying. And I'm not refusing to cooperate with the police! Get out of my yard!

KELLY watches out the window. A few moments later, a key turns in a lock. KELLY drops away from the window and goes to the door to the kitchen. She watches from that vantage point as TEGAN comes into the house and slams her backpack down onto the floor.

KELLY

You lied to me.

TEGAN barely glances at her sister. She heads for the stairs. KELLY rushes at her and grabs her by the arm.

KELLY (CONT'D)
You lied to me. You told me Martin was your boyfriend.

TEGAN wrenches her arm free of Kelly's grip.

TEGAN
If you don't mind, I've already had a crappy day.

KELLY
He wasn't your boyfriend. I heard what Gina said. He wasn't interested in you. He was interested in me. He was going to ask me out.

TEGAN stares stonily at her sister.

KELLY (CONT'D)
You knew it. You knew it, but you pretended you didn't.
(studying her sister's face)
Is Gina right? Is that why you haven't told the police

anything? Because you were mad at Martin? Because you're mad at me?

TEGAN

Martin never said a word to me about you. I have no idea what he really wanted. I don't think *he* knew what he wanted. He was going through a lot of changes.

KELLY
(to the camera)
Changes for the better.

TEGAN

Even if he did plan to ask you out, that doesn't change things. I didn't see who shot him. If I'd seen, I—

KELLY turns her back on her sister.

TEGAN (CONT'D)

Kelly—

KELLY

I can't see you and I can't hear you.

144

TEGAN stares at her sister's back for a moment before running up the stairs to her room. From above, a door slams.

EIGHTEEN

Tegan

I told myself over and over to stay away from my computer. I already knew what people were saying. I'd seen firsthand how they were treating me—including my best friend and my own sister. Why would I want to subject myself to more of the same?

Maybe someone had posted a positive message. Maybe someone was able to see things from my perspective. Maybe someone was actually defending me. I'm not sure I believed it, but that's what I told myself when I logged on to the Internet and pulled up the What Tegan Saw site.

There were a lot of new messages, and they were from all over—from other cities, other states, even a few from

other countries. Some were comments on similar cases—
it was kind of creepy to read about so many people who
had been shot dead in their cars. A couple of those cases
were ones in which there were so-called witnesses who
had, for some reason, been left alive and who had either
cooperated or refused to cooperate with the police. In
one case, the witness committed suicide, which the
person who posted the message said was totally cowardly:
"Rather than see justice done, the jerk-off played right
into the hands of the killer."

Then there was the message that hit me like a kick
in the belly: *$50,000 reward for information leading to the
arrest and conviction of the person or persons responsible for
the death of Martin Genovese.* No questions asked, the
message said. No names, no in-person interviews, just
call the police tips line, give the information, get a special
ID number and collect the money when it's all over.

The reward was being offered by the Genovese family.
It ended with these words: *We pray that anyone with information that can help the police will examine their soul and
do the right thing.*

It made it sound like there was a devil on one shoulder
of that "anyone with information" and an angel on the
other: the first one telling *that person* (as if everyone didn't
know exactly who the Genovese family was referring to)

147

to shut up, save yourself, nothing you can say will bring those boys back to life; and the other one insisting that virtue is its own reward, stand up, tell the truth and trust that you will be protected.

I sat in front of my computer, hitting the Refresh button every now and again, and reading the new posts, a lot of them cynical, asking which was worse: keeping your mouth shut and letting someone get away with murder or collecting a big fat reward for doing what any self-respecting person should have done in a flash because it was the right thing?

My legs wobbled as I approached the construction site on what used to be the site of an auto factory. The factory had been demolished, the land cleaned up, and a new subdivision was going in, built by Genovese Construction. There were gaping holes in the ground in some places, holes filled with concrete foundations in other places, wooden frames of houses in others. One hundred and sixty houses were going to be built, all massive. "My dad's going to make a killing on the project," Martin had told me.

I'd been at the site twice, both times with Martin, both times when he had to stop by to get some cash from his dad. I'd never asked what the cash was for. Now I couldn't help wondering. I stood across the street, scanning the site until I spotted Mr. Genovese in front of one of the wood-framed houses. He was talking to a couple of guys wearing jeans, construction boots and hard hats. I watched him, my heart hammering in my chest. Finally he turned and strode to the trailer that sat at the edge of the site. He went inside.

I waited a moment to see if anyone else was going to go in with him. No one did. I walked haltingly toward the trailer. When I knocked, Mr. Genovese called: "Come!"

I pushed the door open. Mr. Genovese was sitting at the desk in one corner of the trailer, but he got up when he saw me. I don't know what he really thought of me—nothing good, according to Anna—but his eyes lit up and he came toward me as if he were going to hug me.

"You've made a decision," he said. It wasn't a question. He was telling me that he knew why I was here, and he sounded happy about it. There was no contempt in his voice, nothing to make me feel like total garbage for having come to see him only after he had announced a big reward. "You're doing the right thing," he said.

"Mr. Genovese, I had to come. I want to make sure you know. If I'd seen anything, anything at all, that could help the police, I would have told them. I lov—I cared about Martin. A lot. He was my friend. Clark too. But I didn't see anything."

The joy vanished from his face.

"But you were right there," he said. "The police figure you got lucky—the shooter didn't see you because of the tinted glass. But I know what those windows are like. It's hard to see in, but you can see out. Unless you had your eyes shut—"

"They were wide open." I wished they hadn't been. I wished I hadn't seen the surprise on Martin's face. I wish I hadn't seen him draw his last breath.

"Then you saw."

I shook my head. "I'm sorry."

"Maybe you were in shock. What am I saying? Of *course* you were in shock. I talked to some people I know. They say if you tried hypnosis, maybe you'd remember something."

"You don't understand, Mr. Genovese." I wished I'd never come to see him. But he was Martin's dad. I couldn't let him hold out any false hopes that I was going to be able to help him. "I was looking at Martin when it happened. It was so sudden. One minute he was turned around in his seat, smiling at me." Smiling and making me feel like I was the only girl in the world as far as he was concerned, and I'd been willing, even eager, to believe it, even when I knew it wasn't true. "And the next minute—" The next minute I wasn't even sure what I was looking at. A turned head, a look of surprise, blood, Martin slumping forward, the back of his head—which didn't look like a head anymore; it looked like a smashed melon—and more blood...

"I couldn't believe what had happened. It was like I was in some kind of nightmare. I wanted to close my eyes and make it all go away, but I couldn't take my eyes off him. I was looking at him the whole time, Mr. Genovese. I was looking at Martin. I didn't turn my head until it was too late." I hadn't looked at Clark until later either. "I'm sorry, Mr. Genovese. There's no point in hypnotizing me. I didn't see anything."

He towered over me. He was a tall man, like Martin, and powerfully built. He looked like he could do everything any man on one of his construction crews could do, and when things got tight, when deadlines were closing in, he probably pitched in. I saw his arm muscles flex as his hands curled into fists.

"There's a reward," he said. "Fifty grand."

"I know."

"That's a lot of money. It could pay for your education."

"I wish I could help you, but I can't."

"I'll make it a hundred grand."

"Mr. Genovese—"

"A hundred and fifty. You were there. You were in the car with him. You saw my boy die. I understand if you're scared. If he'd lived, Marty would probably be scared too. But he'd do the right thing. He'd step forward."

"I'm sorry."

I turned and opened the trailer door.

"Two hundred grand."

I stepped outside. He appeared in the door behind me.

"Name your price," he called as I ran down the stairs. "Tell me what you want. Anything!"

I ran until I was out of sight of the subdivision-to-be. When I got home, I unplugged my computer. I didn't want to know what people were saying. I didn't want to know anything else about it.

NINETEEN
Kelly

EXT.—SIDEWALK IN FRONT OF THE
HIGH SCHOOL—DAY

KELLY is standing on the sidewalk with LACEY. Kids are streaming out of school. Classes are over for the day.

> LACEY
>
> If I were her, I'd have caved by now. You know Carly Jessup and Andrea Cornish?

> KELLY
>
> Sure. They're tight with Anna Genovese.

LACEY

They're also talking about freezing Tegan out for the rest of the year. You know how popular Clark and Martin were—especially Martin. People are never going to forgive her for what she's doing.

KELLY

What if she's telling the truth? What if she *didn't* see anything?

LACEY

Do you believe that?

KELLY

I don't know what to believe.
(to the camera)
She's my sister. I should be sticking up for her. But you know how they say familiarity breeds contempt? Well, that's because the more familiar you are with someone, the more you know about her, the clearer it is to you when she's not exactly a saint. Tegan isn't a bad person. But she is a little self-absorbed. What am I saying? She's completely self-absorbed. And she's capable of being really vindictive. She adored Martin. She talked about him all the time. All she

ever wanted was to go out with him—and it turns out he just thought of her as a pal. It turns out he was more interested in me. I can see Tegan getting really mad about that. I hate to say it, but it's true. And I can see her taking it out on Martin—and me—by keeping her mouth shut about what she saw. It's a terrible thing to have to say about your sister, but it's the way I feel.

LACEY

Uh-oh.

LACEY points, and KELLY turns to see ANNA break away from a group of girls and come toward her. KELLY groans.

KELLY

Now what?

ANNA

Your sister went to see my dad this morning.

KELLY looks surprised, even though she is trying not to show it.

KELLY

So?

ANNA

My dad's offering a reward for information leading to the arrest of Martin's killer.

KELLY

I heard.

ANNA

Your sister went to see him. She told him that she couldn't help him.

KELLY

What's that got to do with me?

ANNA

It's your birthday in a couple of days, isn't it?

KELLY

Yeah. So?

ANNA

Martin was going to ask you out. He really liked you.

KELLY
(looking uncomfortable)
He never said anything to me about that.

ANNA
You liked him, didn't you?

KELLY nods.

ANNA (CONT'D)
A lot?

KELLY
(softly)
Yeah.

ANNA digs in her pocket and brings out a small box.

ANNA
I went shopping with Martin before he died. He
wanted to get something for your birthday. And he
made me go with him because he wanted to buy
you the perfect thing. But he wouldn't listen to any
suggestions I made. He ended up buying this.

ANNA hands the box to KELLY, who opens it with trembling fingers. Nestled on cotton batting in the small box is a delicate chain with a little gold charm—it's a dolphin. KELLY smiles.

> ANNA (CONT'D)
> He said it was because you're a swimmer. Because you're a good one.

> KELLY
> It's perfect.

KELLY stares into the box for a moment, then replaces the lid and holds it out to Anna. ANNA shakes her head.

> ANNA
> He bought it for you.

KELLY hesitates. Finally she slips the little box into her pocket.

> ANNA (CONT'D)
> Your sister is letting Martin's killer get away with murder.

KELLY

Maybe she's telling the truth. Maybe she really didn't
see anything.

ANNA

Maybe? It sounds like you don't believe her any more
than I do.

KELLY eyes Anna with suspicion, torn between believing
her and feeling that she should support her sister, no
matter how unworthy of support she might be.

ANNA (CONT'D)

She knew how Martin felt about you.

KELLY

So?

ANNA

Did she tell you she knew?

KELLY doesn't answer.

ANNA (CONT'D)

I didn't think so.

KELLY

Just because she might have been angry at Martin,
that doesn't mean she would let his murderer go free.

ANNA

What if she knew that what happened was her
fault—and she knew who did it and was terrified
that if she opened her mouth, he would come after
her?

KELLY

What do you mean, her fault?

ANNA looks at Lacey. Then she pulls Kelly down the
block where no one else can hear what she says.

ANNA
(dropping her voice)
I know Martin was into smoking weed.

KELLY

I know. I also know you knew he got busted for it.

ANNA is stunned.

KELLY (CONT'D)

But you gave Tegan a hard time because the cops went
to your house and said that to your parents. You made
it sound like it was all a great big lie.

ANNA

Did your mom know Tegan was into weed?

KELLY
(reluctantly)
No.

ANNA

My parents were destroyed when the cops showed
up at my house and told them that Martin had been
shot. Shot! What kind of people shoot people? What
kind of people get shot?

KELLY
(to the camera)
Gangsters shoot people. Most people who get shot are
leading what the cops call high-risk lifestyles, which
is just a diplomatic way of saying if you hang around
with people who have guns, don't be surprised if one
day one of them shoots you.

ANNA

He just liked to smoke up now and again. Is that such a crime? Okay, so maybe technically it is. But all this stuff about dealing—yeah, so maybe Martin bought a little more than he needed for himself. But that's because people bugged him. They knew he knew who to get it from. But when he got busted—he did what they told him. He did a program. He got out of it. It wasn't easy, you know. He got a lot of pressure from kids who were used to him having stuff. Like your sister. He really tried to stick to his promise. He said he didn't want to disappoint you.

KELLY stares at her, slightly stunned.

ANNA (CONT'D)

I told him to stay out of it too, but it mattered more to him what you said. I think he was relieved to have someone like you in his life. He wanted a reason, a good one, for when his friends pressured him. And, anyway, I think he was getting scared.

KELLY

What do you mean?

ANNA

The cops tried to scare him when they busted him.
They said the drug scene was getting fierce—they
said there were new players, more ruthless ones. But
I think he already knew that. He told me once that
the new guy he bought from scared him. He said
he'd been wondering if it was worth it. But he had all
those friends, and he was *their* connection. That's the
only reason he didn't quit earlier. He needed you on
his side, Kelly. He needed someone who believed in
him and who supported him.

KELLY

Do you know who his connection was?

ANNA shakes her head.

KELLY (CONT'D)

Did you tell the cops what you just told me?

ANNA

Yeah.
(hesitates for a moment)
He was through. And then Tegan started in on him.

163

KELLY

What do you mean?

ANNA

She must have called him a dozen times. He told me. She kept saying, just one more time. One more time. Martin's a good guy—*was* a good guy. If you ask me, he was too nice. He tried too hard to make everyone happy.

KELLY

Are you saying he was killed because of Tegan?

ANNA

Think about it. The cops can't come up with anyone who had a motive for shooting Martin—except his drug connection. But he wouldn't have had a drug connection anymore if it wasn't for your sister. And who knows what really happened that night. Who knows if it even happened the way she said it did. She was the only witness. A lot of things could have happened, but nobody will ever know unless she decides to cooperate with the cops.

KELLY is silent. She looks stunned, as if she is having trouble absorbing this new information.

ANNA (CONT'D)
You have to help me, Kelly. You have to turn up the heat on her. You have to tell her that you know she was the one who pushed Martin to buy drugs that night. You have to make it clear to her that nothing is going to change until she does the right thing. You can't let Martin's killer get away with it. You can't.

TWENTY

Tegan

The one good thing about a crappy day—you can tell your-self that things can't get any worse, and ninety-eight times out of a hundred, you're right. The other two times out of a hundred? Well, here's how my crappy day unfolded:

After paying a visit to Mr. Genovese, I went to school, where nobody except teachers would look at me, much less talk to me. And the whole time I was there, I couldn't stop thinking about all those people who had left posts on that website; people who didn't even know me but who thought I was the lowest form of life on the planet—a coward who refused to avenge her friends' deaths. After home form, I found myself walking around with my head down. What was the point of looking at people who were only going to look away from me? I stared at my toes, I stared at the floor, I stared at my desk, I stared at my textbooks and notebooks. I was focused on the interlocking cement blocks that made up the broad walkway in front of school when two mirror-shiny shoes appeared right in front of me.

"Tegan?"

This is where my day pulled a two-percenter—it took a turn for the crappier.

It was Mr. Deacon. His smile came across like a muscle spasm, like he hadn't planned it, like it had happened involuntarily. There was no real feeling behind it that I could see.

"I'd like to buy you a soda," he said, his voice as smooth as a freshly paved road, easing the way for me to say yes. Did he think I was brain-dead? The last time I'd seen him, he had practically accused me of being in league with the killer.

"No, thanks." I didn't even try to sound polite. Why should I? I tried to circle around him, but he blocked my way.

"Please? There's a little place just over there." He pointed to a café across the street from school.

"I hate that place," I said. At least, I did now. Martin liked the lattes over there. He always ordered a huge bowl.

Lately I'd been going with him. But remembering Martin wasn't the only thing that made me never want to go there again. The café was also a place where kids from my school hung out.

"Name the place then," Mr. Deacon said. "It's important, Tegan. We need to talk."

"About what?"

"I thought you might like an update on what's been happening."

An update?

I glanced around.

"How about over there?" I nodded at a tiny greasy spoon with grimy windows. There was no chance I'd run into anyone from my school there.

He stared at the place. I was sure he was going to reject it, and then we'd have to negotiate. I wanted to hear whatever news he had, but I didn't want to spend any more time with him than I had to. Besides, if there was news, I could always get it from Detective Zorbas.

But he didn't reject my suggestion. He nodded, and we set off across the street. He had his phone out by the time we got to the door.

"I'm sorry," he said. "I have to take this. I'll be right in."

I hadn't heard his phone ring, so I guessed he had it on vibrate. I pushed the door open and stepped onto worn,

cracked linoleum. The place didn't look like much—
tables without tablecloths, mismatched chairs, the
menu items displayed in faded artwork over the counter
on a back-lit sheet of plastic. The only customers were
a couple of old men at the back of the place hunched over
bottles of beer. I grabbed a table as far as possible from
both the window and the beer drinkers and waited for
Mr. Deacon.

He came through the door a moment later and looked
around with the curiosity of an anthropologist. I ordered
tea. He followed my lead, and we sat in silence until it
was delivered in little metal teapots that leaked when you
tried to pour them.

"So?" I said when he still hadn't said anything.

The door to the restaurant opened and he turned.
A man and a woman came in. They both stopped
and gazed around, open-mouthed, until they located
Mr. Deacon. The woman's nose wrinkled in disapproval.

"No way," I said, standing up.

Mr. Deacon grabbed my wrist and held me.

"I'm sorry," he said. "But I didn't think you'd agree to
talk if you knew they were going to be here."

"You were right." I tried to pull free, but his grip was
too strong.

"You owe it to them to talk to them, Tegan."

Mrs. Carson slipped her hand through her husband's arm and he led her to our table. He pulled out a chair for her and dusted it with a handkerchief he produced from his pants pocket. She sat gingerly on the edge. A waitress appeared, but Mrs. Carson waved her away without a word. No way was she going to touch anything in this place.

Mr. Carson fixed me with piercing gray eyes that were just like Clark's.

"I'm going to come right to the point," he said. "I'm not here to offer a reward. Maybe some believe in bribes to get people to do what they should be doing in the first place, but I don't. I'm here to put it to you plainly. You witnessed my son's murder. For whatever reason, you are insisting that, although you couldn't have been more than a couple of feet away from the killer, you saw nothing. If it were up to me, you would be charged with obstruction of justice, but apparently that isn't an option. So I'm just going to put the facts to you. Fact one, my son did not do drugs."

I opened my mouth to say something, but he cut me off.

"Yes, I am aware that there was one time when he came home under the influence," he said. "He experimented.

All young people experiment. But that was that. It never happened again."

The way Clark had told it, his parents had screamed at him for a solid hour because of what had happened to his brother Scott. Scott had experimented with drugs too. But the experiment had turned into a more-or-less permanent state, which, coupled with an expensive car, had led to a crash and a spinal-cord injury. Scott was never going to walk again. He didn't talk very well either.

So when Clark came home giggling like a fool and reeking of weed, Mr. Carson had forbidden him to associate with Martin. They had a huge fight over that. Then Mr. Carson brought out the big guns—he promised that he would disinherit Clark if he ever touched drugs again. Mr. Carson must have been quite a piece of work. He must have been one of those guys who never makes a threat he doesn't intend to keep, because Clark caved. He said it wasn't worth it to have to pass a sniff test every time he got home. In return, his father gave way on the issue of Martin. Neither of his parents liked Martin, but Clark never stopped being his friend. He did stop using drugs though—not that it killed his party life, because alcohol was a whole different story. Mr. Carson had nothing against alcohol. In fact, he figured that since kids are going to drink anyway, they might as well do it at home, on the theory that it would lead to responsible drinking. Clark's parents scolded him when he got drunk, but it was nothing like the way they acted about weed. Not even close. The time he got totally wasted and drove his car into the stone wall around the property, his father actually said to him, "Well, that's something you won't ever do again." Clark said his mother freaked out—what if he'd been killed or, worse, permanently disabled like his brother? What if he'd killed someone else? But did they refuse to buy him a new car? No. Did they restrict his right to drive? No. Did they cut off his supply of alcohol? Uh-uh. It was business as usual.

They also didn't freak when Clark racked up speeding tickets, and once—it was amazing it was only once— a ticket for reckless driving when he kept weaving through traffic on the highway to get ahead, get ahead, get ahead. He always wanted to be out front, and he never cared who he cut off or freaked out while he did it. If someone flipped him the finger, he returned the gesture and left them in the dust. But that probably wouldn't have mattered to Mr. Carson, if he had known about it. He probably would have said that Clark was just blowing off steam.

"Fact two," Mr. Carson said, "my son did nothing to bring this on himself—except maybe exercise poor judgment in deciding, against the advice and wishes of both his mother and myself, to continue his association with Martin Genovese. Fact three, it was Martin Genovese's involvement with the drug trade that led to my son's death."

Fact?

"I thought that was just a theory," I said. "I thought the police weren't sure."

Mrs. Carson stared at me like I was a slug on one of her prize roses.

"It's their only avenue of investigation," Mr. Carson said. "You tell me what that means. Fact four, you were in that car. It is within your power to provide the police with some kind of investigative lead. As I say, there's nothing the police can charge you with because, they tell me, there's no solid evidence that you are engaging in obstruction. But I promise you this, young lady. If you don't do *something* to assist the police in arresting my son's killer, I can and will make your life very unpleasant. You know what I do, don't you, Tegan?"

What he *did*?

"You mean, for a living?"

He nodded.

"I know you own some companies." Everyone knew it.

"Do you know which ones?"

I shook my head. Clark had said something once about a holding company, which, when I asked, he said was a company that owned other companies. He'd mentioned a couple of names that I sort of recognized too, although I wasn't sure what they did. Plus there was a bakery that Mrs. Carson had started up. It got a lot of press because all of the profits that didn't get plowed back into the business were donated to charity.

"Well, among others, I own a company that controls the company where your mother works."

Right then I knew what he was going to say next. He didn't disappoint me.

"You know the economy is in a bit of a mess right now, don't you?" he said. "A lot of places have been letting people go. It would be a shame if your mother were to lose her job."

I couldn't believe it. I glanced at Mrs. Carson, who all of a sudden didn't look like a person who was interested in charity, and at Mr. Deacon.

"Are you threatening me, Mr. Carson?" I said.

"No, I'm not, as I'm sure Mrs. Carson and Mr. Deacon will be able to attest. Besides, I have no direct say over the day-to-day operations of the company."

Right. But I bet he had plenty of indirect say.

"Think about it, Tegan," he said. He stood up and reached out an arm to help his wife. Mr. Deacon threw some money onto the table to pay for the tea that neither of us had touched. They all walked out of the restaurant together.

I was shaking as I looked across the table at Detective Zorbas an hour later.

"I'll talk to Mr. Carson when I get a chance, Tegan," he said.

"But he can't really do it, can he? He can't get my mother fired—can he?"

"He shouldn't have threatened to have her removed from her job because of you. But the economy is in a mess right now, and if other people are let go at the same time...He's upset. But I will talk to him."

I hesitated before I asked the next question.

"He said you're pretty sure the shooting was drug-related."

"I wouldn't say that we're sure of anything at the moment." He ran down the facts for me. Maybe I'm stupid, but it had never occurred to me that the police wouldn't be able to find whoever killed Clark and Martin. If it was TV or the movies, they'd come up with something. But Detective Zorbas seemed genuinely stumped. No shell casings. No fingerprints. No hairs. No fibers. No footwear impressions. No one saw anyone in the street. No one saw anyone running away from the scene. No one saw a car driving away from the scene. No one knew of anyone who had been in a fight or an argument with either Clark or Martin. No one knew anyone who had a grudge against either of them. The cops had absolutely zero leads.

"The one thing we do know is that Martin was involved with drugs," Detective Zorbas said. "I thought he'd learned his lesson, but…"

Learned his lesson?

"What do you mean?"

Detective Zorbas looked evenly at me. "He didn't tell you?"

"Tell me what?"

"About the time he was arrested. For drugs."

"Martin was arrested?" No, that couldn't be right. If Martin had been arrested, I would have heard about it. The whole school would have heard about it.

"It was six—no, seven months ago. He was arrested. I gather he called his buddy Clark, and Clark called his father, and some kind of deal was made. Charges were dropped on condition that Martin successfully complete a drug rehab program."

"Rehab?" No way! "You make it sound like he was a junkie or a meth-head or something."

"He was dealing drugs, Tegan."

"He was getting stuff for his friends from time to time. That didn't make him a drug dealer."

"That's splitting hairs, and I think you know it. He was getting drugs from a dealer and was reselling them to his friends. According to the law, that's dealing. I know he went to the program. I know he quit drugs."

Was that why Martin had turned serious all of a sudden? Was that why he never wanted to party anymore? Because he'd got caught and had made a deal?

"But apparently that didn't stick. He smoked up the night he was killed."

God, and it was probably because of me. I'd been after him—*Come on, Martin, stop being such a bore. Let's have some fun. Get some stuff. For me? Please? I'm tired from all that studying. It's a party. We're* supposed *to unwind.* I'd seen that look on his face. I had the feeling he was going to say no, and it pissed me off. What was wrong with him?

Now I knew.

And that night—he'd handed the stuff to me. He'd said, "Here. A present." And he'd looked deep into my eyes. He'd said, "I have to talk to you, Tegan." And, stupid me, I thought he was going to tell me that he was interested in me, that we made a great couple, that we should be together. He'd seemed nervous, and guys are always nervous when they're about to declare themselves. I mean, there's always the chance of rejection, right? But maybe that wasn't what he'd been nervous about, at least not according to Gina. Maybe he was going to drive a knife through my heart. Maybe he was going to tell me how he felt about Kelly. Maybe that's why he was nervous. Jeez, it was probably why he'd finally said yes after months of being a total stick-in-the-mud.

It was probably why he'd finally caved and smoked a joint with me after telling me half the night that he wasn't interested.

"The drug scene is changing, Tegan," Detective Zorbas said. "Some of the players now, they're not so nice, if you know what I mean. He knew that. We thought he understood—kids who get involved with drugs often end up knowing the wrong kind of people. People with guns. We've been working on trying to find out who Martin's connection was, but so far we've come up empty."

He peered somberly at me. "Do you have any idea where he got the stuff?"

"I never asked. I guess I didn't want to know."

He crossed his arms over his chest and studied me for a few moments.

"The gangs that run drugs in this city aren't stupid," he said at last. "They're criminals, but they're sophisticated. They read the papers. They listen to the news. They're on the Internet."

I frowned. What was he getting at?

"We didn't release your name, Tegan. That's not something we do. But it's all over the media. And the Net. You know what I'm saying?"

"You mean, they know who I am?"

"Whoever did it knows you haven't told us anything. They know that so far they've gotten away with murder. We're pretty good at what we do here, Tegan. But a lot of times, contrary to what you see on TV, we have to rely on ordinary people to help us. People like you. People who saw something or heard something or who know something—anything at all. People like that can give us the edge we need. When there are people like that around, we end up making an arrest. Then there are cases like this one—when it's gang-related and people are too scared to come forward. I understand why people are afraid, Tegan. But unless someone is willing to stand up, we've got nothing. The killer goes free. The gangs continue. They know they can intimidate people, and that's exactly what they do. It makes the city—your city, Tegan— a worse place to live in."

"I didn't see anything," I said for what seemed like the millionth time. "Why doesn't anyone believe me?"

"All I'm asking you to do is think it over. Think about the times Martin had drugs on him. Do you remember him saying where he might have got them? Did he mention a name? How did he find his connection? Did someone at school hook him up? Did he ever mention he had to go somewhere, maybe to get something? It might seem like it isn't important, but it could make all the difference. Just think about it, okay, Tegan? Think about it and let me know if you come up with anything."

I said that I would. But I felt like a fraud because I didn't know anything.

I was pretty shook up when I left the police station. The killer knew who I was. He knew what school I went to. He knew what I looked like—my picture was on the What Tegan Saw website. He also knew that the police had been questioning me. What if he started to get nervous about what I had seen? What if he started to stalk me, waiting to get me alone? What if he decided to make sure that I never said anything? What if…?

I slammed awake in the middle of the night, my heart racing, a silent scream echoing in my head. I had just been face-to-face with Martin's and Clark's killer. He was in the shadows, so I hadn't been able to make out much—just a long black smudge against the black of the shadow. I couldn't see his face, but I heard his voice. He was laughing.

He was laughing because he had killed two people and had gotten away with it.

Because there had been someone else in the car when he'd pulled that trigger, and so far that person—me—hadn't said a word to the police.

He was laughing at me because he had scared me into silence, and everyone knew it.

He was laughing at how terrified I was, because my terror guaranteed his freedom.

He was laughing at scared little me.

TWENTY-ONE

Kelly

INT.—TYRELL KITCHEN—NIGHT

KELLY and MRS. TYRELL are seated at a small table in the kitchen. Each has a plate of food in front of her. Each is pushing that food around the plate, but neither is eating. MRS. TYRELL keeps staring at the ceiling. KELLY stares out into space. She fingers the charm on a gold chain around her neck.

> **MRS. TYRELL**
>
> She's been up there ever since she got home from school. She's so upset. I know something happened, but she won't tell me what.

KELLY says nothing. She isn't listening to her mother.

> MRS. TYRELL (CONT'D)
> Well? Do you know?

> KELLY
> Huh?

> MRS. TYRELL
> You were at the same school all day. You must have heard something or seen something. Are people giving her a hard time?

> KELLY
> I don't know. I have my own life, Mom. My own problems.

KELLY gets up with her plate, scrapes the food on it into the garbage and sets the plate into the sink.

> KELLY (CONT'D)
> I have homework.

KELLY leaves the kitchen.

CUT TO:

INT.-TYRELL UPSTAIRS HALLWAY-NIGHT

KELLY comes up the stairs and starts downs the hall to her own room. She pauses in front of a closed door— the door to Tegan's room. She stares at it. It is silent in the hall. She raises a hand and reaches for the doorknob. She seems frozen for a moment. She drops her hand and continues down the hall to her own room. She enters.

CUT TO:

INT.-KELLY'S ROOM-NIGHT

KELLY is sitting on her bed, staring at her now-closed door.

> KELLY
> (to the camera)

If Anna is right and the cops are right, then it was Tegan's fault. Martin got out of drugs. He did a whole rehab program. He didn't even want to be involved anymore. But Tegan wouldn't leave him alone. She kept bugging him. I bet some of the others did too. Some of his so-called friends who used him to get their supply.

She stands up and walks to her door. Her hand goes out again, just as it did when she was standing in front of

Tegan's room a few moments earlier. Once again, she drops her hand.

KELLY (CONT'D)

But would she really let Martin's murderer get away with it? Maybe she would, if she was scared enough. I mean, I guess the cops could offer to protect her, but if the guy who did it is part of a gang, then, really, what can they do? It's not like they're going to assign cops to her 24/7. They don't have the manpower for that. And those gangs have a long memory. So, yeah, maybe she's afraid. Maybe I'd be afraid if I was in her place.

She turns and goes back to her bed. She sits, her hands clasped in her lap.

KELLY (CONT'D)

But what's that saying? I don't remember it exactly, but it's something like the only thing you need for evil to win is for good people to do nothing. If Tegan saw something, even if she's afraid, she should do the right thing. Otherwise, Martin's killer gets away with murder. Maybe she's got another reason for saying nothing.

Her fingers go to the chain around her neck.

KELLY (CONT'D)

Maybe she was mad at Martin—because of me.
Maybe her way of getting even with him is to do
nothing. Is that possible? Is my sister really that kind
of person?

TWENTY-TWO

Tegan

I told myself, Calm down. I told myself, It's going to be okay.

But it wasn't.

How could it be?

Nobody believed me when I said I hadn't seen who did it.

Nobody would speak to me. Nobody would even look at me.

Clark's dad was threatening to get my mother fired from her job.

Detective Zorbas said that whoever had done it probably knew everything about me—where I lived, where I went to school…where to find me. What he was trying to tell me was, That guy is out there, and he's out there because you haven't done anything about it.

But what was I supposed to do?

What was I supposed to do?

I have no idea how long I sat on my bed asking myself the same question over and over.

I still couldn't believe how everything had changed so fast. One day my life was normal and I was happy. Midterms were over, I was doing my favorite thing— having fun kicking back with my friends—and the way Martin was looking at me, I was sure Gina was wrong. Martin wasn't interested in Kelly; he was interested in me. I was even more sure of it on the way back to the car when he stumbled and put an arm around my waist and told me he thought I was gorgeous—drop-dead gorgeous. I couldn't wait to get into Clark's car. I wanted to get to my house. I wanted Martin to get out of the car and walk me up to my porch. I wanted him to pull me close to him and kiss me. It was going to happen. I knew it was.

And then everything changed.

Now Martin was dead, and everyone hated me because I wasn't doing anything about it. But what was I supposed to do?

Then, *bang*, like the shot that had started it all, there was the answer.

I jumped up off the bed and opened the door to my room. I walked down the hall to Kelly's room. She hated me more than anyone else, but I needed her help. I rapped on her door.

"What?" she snarled from inside.

"I need to talk to you."

There was silence for a few moments, but then her door opened.

"What?" she said again. She was scowling at me.

"I need your help."

She stared at me and started to close her door. I put out my hands to stop her.

"Please, Kel? It's important."

"Martin is dead because of you."

"I know."

Her scowl vanished, but her suspicion didn't.

"What do you want?"

"Your webcam."

"What for?"

"Can I use it or not, Kel?"

She stared at me. "You don't know how."

"So show me. You're always telling me how easy it is." Actually, the way she put it was that she didn't understand how I couldn't do something even an untrained monkey could figure out.

It took a few moments, but she finally stepped aside to let me in.

"What are you up to, Teeg?"

"Just show me how to use it, okay, Kel? And how to post what I shoot."

"Does this have something to do with Martin?"

"Show me and I'll owe you big-time. Anything you want, anytime you want."

Another few moments ticked by. I was afraid she was going to say no.

Instead, she said, "Sit down."

I sat in front of her computer. She pulled a chair up beside me.

"Okay," she said, "here's how the camera works."

She had to show me a couple of times and got exasperated with me, as usual, but I finally felt confident I knew what I was doing. Then she sank down on her bed cross-legged. She was planning to watch me.

"Um, I sort of need privacy," I said.

"If you want privacy, you should go to your own room."

"Please, Kel?" I had never begged so much from her in my whole life.

"Fine," she said. She slammed out of her room, and I heard her feet as she stomped down the stairs. I heard Mom, too, asking if a herd of elephants had broken into the house.

I got up and closed the door. Then I sat in front of the computer and got to work.

TWENTY-THREE
Kelly

INT.—TYRELL LIVING ROOM—DAY

KELLY is curled up on the sofa, sound asleep in front
of the TV, which is on, the sound turned down low.
She stirs. Her eyes open a little. She stretches. Slowly,
she sits up. Yawning, she reaches for the TV remote and
flicks to a news channel, where she sees the time that is
shown on the bottom right-hand corner of the screen.
It is 6:00 AM. She flicks the TV off, stands and stretches
more fully, arms over her head, arcing just enough to
stretch out her back. She scratches, runs her tongue
over her teeth and makes a sour face. She heads for
the stairs.

CUT TO:

INT.-TYRELL UPSTAIRS HALLWAY-DAY

KELLY appears at the top of the stairs and starts down the hall to her own room. She pauses at Tegan's room, opens the door and peeks inside. Tegan is not there. Her bed is made. KELLY frowns. She continues to her own room and opens that door. Tegan is not there either.

CUT TO:

INT.-KELLY'S BEDROOM-DAY

KELLY stumbles across the room to her bed. She is sinking down onto it when she realizes that her computer is still on. She goes over to her computer table and sits down. She sees a piece of scrap paper with something scribbled on it—the URL for the What Tegan Saw website. Frowning, KELLY clicks on the site and sees that a video has been posted. She clicks on it to watch. Close-up on computer screen. TEGAN's face appears. Looking directly out from the screen, TEGAN speaks.

TEGAN

My name is Tegan Tyrell. I was in the car with Clark Carson and Martin Genovese when they were shot dead. People have been saying that I must have seen whoever shot my friends.

193

Close-up on KELLY's face. KELLY stares at the screen.

>   TEGAN'S VOICE
>   (off camera)
> People have been saying that the reason I haven't told
> the police what I know about who did it is because
> I'm afraid that if I do, the killer will come after me.
> They say I'm afraid.

Close-up on computer screen and TEGAN's face.

>   TEGAN
> I've given a lot of thought to what people have been
> saying and why they've been saying it. I know it's
> because they loved Clark and Martin. I understand
> that. I respect that. I want everyone to know that I'm
> not afraid. Maybe I was—I can't begin to tell you
> what it's like to see what I saw that night. I couldn't
> sleep for days. I kept seeing...

TEGAN's voice breaks off and, for once, her gaze wavers.
She looks down for a second before staring into the
camera again.

TEGAN (CONT'D)

I'm not afraid. This video is for the person who shot Clark and Martin. I'm going to assume that you're a human being. I'm going to assume that on some level, in some small way, you regret what you did. So I'm going to give you until sunrise tomorrow morning to do the right thing—surrender to the police. If I don't hear from the police that you've given yourself up, then I am going to go to the police myself and tell them who you are. I'm not afraid anymore. I'm going to do the right thing.

KELLY stares at the screen. She stands up slowly. She grabs her cell phone.

CUT TO:

INT.—TYRELL UPSTAIRS HALLWAY—DAY

KELLY bursts out of her room and dashes down to Tegan's room. She peers inside again as if hoping her sister has miraculously materialized, but she hasn't. She stares at the clock on Tegan's bedside table. Then she runs downstairs, shoves her feet into a pair of slip-on sneakers, grabs a jacket and runs outside.

CUT TO:

EXT.-STREET IN FRONT OF TYRELL HOUSE-DAY

KELLY is on the street, looking frantically first one way and then the other. She sees no one. She runs in one direction.

CUT TO:

EXT.-STREET CORNER-DAY

KELLY is panting as she reaches the corner of her street. She pauses for a moment to look both ways again.

> KELLY
> (shouting)

Tegan!

KELLY pulls her cell phone out of her pocket and punches in 9-1-1. She runs while she talks into the phone. She reaches another corner.

CUT TO:

EXT.-SECOND STREET CORNER-DAY

KELLY grinds to a stop and lets the phone drop from her ear. Up ahead, two full blocks away, is TEGAN. She is walking at an even pace. KELLY breathes a sigh of relief.

KELLY
(into the phone)
Never mind. False alarm.

KELLY pockets her phone and picks up the pace, going after her sister. As she does, a black van pulls around a corner up ahead. It moves slowly and almost silently down the deserted street. As KELLY watches, the driver's-side window descends. Something glints in the rising sun.

CUT TO:

EXT.–STREET–DAY

TEGAN turns toward the van. Her eyes widen and her mouth forms a large O. She spins around and starts to run away from the van. There is a muffled sound. TEGAN crumples onto the sidewalk.

CUT TO:

EXT.–STREET–DAY

Close-up on KELLY. She screams.

CUT TO:

EXT.–STREET–DAY

The van roars down the street, rounds a corner and vanishes from sight.

CUT TO:

INT.—HOSPITAL WAITING ROOM—DAY

KELLY and MRS. TYRELL are seated in the waiting room. Both look exhausted. MRS. TYRELL drinks coffee from a paper cup. KELLY is on her cell phone. DET. ZORBAS arrives. KELLY watches him speak to a nurse.

> KELLY
> (into the phone)
> Anna, I gotta go. I'll talk to you later.

DET. ZORBAS approaches Kelly and Mrs. Tyrell.

> DET. ZORBAS
> Mrs. Tyrell? They tell me Tegan should be out of surgery soon.

MRS. TYRELL looks up at him with weary reddened eyes. DET. ZORBAS squeezes her shoulder. He looks at Kelly.

> DET. ZORBAS (CONT'D)
> I understand you saw the whole thing.

KELLY nods.

DET. ZORBAS (CONT'D)

We need to talk, Kelly.

        (glancing around)

Come on.

KELLY stands. She follows him to a distant, unoccupied corner of the waiting room and takes the chair he indicates. He pulls up a chair opposite her.

DET. ZORBAS (CONT'D)

I need you to tell me exactly what happened.

KELLY

I told the cops who showed up. I told them everything I remembered about the van and the driver. Did they find him?

DET. ZORBAS

They're looking. You've been a big help, Kelly, with the description of the car and the partial plate. (pause) Kelly, I need you to tell me everything you told them. I need you to tell me everything you remember.

KELLY

She came into my room last night. She said she

wanted to use my webcam. She wanted me to show her how. She made a video. She posted it. She said she wasn't afraid to tell the police who shot Martin and Clark. She said she was going to go to the police if the guy didn't turn himself in.

KELLY looks at Det. Zorbas, a weary expression on her face.

KELLY (CONT'D)

He never would have given himself up. Why did she think he would?

DET. ZORBAS
(frowning)

What do you mean, he never would have given himself up? Do you know this person?

KELLY nods.

KELLY

I saw him at the dentist that time. Clark stole his parking space and the guy threatened Clark. He had these two pit bulls with him. He was really mean-looking.

DET. ZORBAS

And this is the guy who shot Tegan?

KELLY

It was his car. I recognized it. It's a black Lexus van. I didn't get the whole license plate, but I got some of it. And I saw one of the dogs.

DET. ZORBAS

Did you see the driver? Did you see him when he shot Tegan?

KELLY shakes her head.

KELLY

But it was his car. And his dog. It was him. I just talked to Anna Genovese. She was with Clark one time—with Clark and Martin. She told me they were walking down the street and Clark saw this van, and he keyed it. She said it was an expensive van— a black Lexus. It was the same guy. And there were two pit bulls in the car.

A cell phone trills. DET. ZORBAS pulls a phone out of his pocket and looks at the display.

> DET. ZORBAS
> (standing)
> Excuse me. I have to take this.

DET. ZORBAS steps away from Kelly and turns his back to get as much privacy as possible for his call. He is grim-faced when he returns.

> DET. ZORBAS (CONT'D)
> They found the van—and the driver. They took him in for questioning. I need you to tell me again, Kelly. Tell me everything you remember about this guy.

CUT TO:

INT.—HOSPITAL ROOM—NIGHT

KELLY and MRS. TYRELL are sitting close to Tegan's bed, watching and waiting. Neither speaks. Both are one-hundred-percent focused on TEGAN, who stirs. MRS. TYRELL sits forward and touches her daughter's hand. TEGAN opens her eyes. MRS. TYRELL squeezes her hand as tears run down her cheeks.

> MRS. TYRELL
> The doctor says you're going to be okay. He says you were very lucky.

TEGAN attempts a smile. She closes her eyes for a moment and then opens them again.

KELLY

They got the guy, Teeg. The guy who shot Martin and Clark and you. They got him.

TEGAN nods, but the movement is almost imperceptible. She closes her eyes.

TWENTY-FOUR
Tegan

Detective Zorbas came to see me the day after I was shot. He had pictures for me to look at, a couple of pages of them, six to a page.

"I know you probably don't feel like it right now, Tegan," he said, "but I need you to look at these and tell me if you recognize anyone."

My mouth was dry. My throat was sore. The nurse told me this was because they had put a respirator in me. But I didn't feel much pain, mainly because they had me on super-strength painkillers. I nodded.

Detective Zorbas stood close to the bed and showed me the first six photographs. I looked carefully at each one and shook my head. He showed me another six photographs. Right away I zeroed in on one of the faces.

"That one," I said. I tried to lift my arm to point, but I couldn't. I was too stiff, and my arm was too heavy. "The one at the bottom in the middle," I said. The one with the thin face and the long black hair. The one with the thin lips like a line across the bottom of his face, and the scar, and the small piercing eyes, looking out at the camera like he didn't give a damn that he was under arrest. The one whose face I had seen when I heard the van beside me and turned to see who it was. The last face I saw before I woke up in the hospital to see my mother in tears.

"You're sure?" Detective Zorbas said.

I nodded. "He's the one who shot me."

"That's good, Tegan." He took out a pen and helped me hold it so that I could put my initials next to the photograph I had picked out. He slipped all of the photographs back into a brown envelope. "Is he also the one who shot Clark and Martin?"

"I guess so."

"You guess? You're not sure?"

"He must be," I said. "He shot me."

"You didn't recognize him from the night Clark and Martin were killed?"

I shook my head. Bad idea. Right away the whole room started to spin. I felt like I was going to throw up.

"I didn't see who shot them. I didn't see anything."

"But your video…"

"You said whoever did it had probably seen that website. You said…" My mouth was so dry. My throat was so sore. I tried to reach for the glass of water with the straw in it that was sitting on my bedside table. Detective Zorbas saw what I was trying to do. He picked up the glass and slipped the end of the straw into my mouth. He put the glass back onto the table when I had finished.

"The gun we found at his place is the same gun that was used to shoot Clark and Martin. You took a big chance, Tegan. If your sister hadn't followed you…"

"Everybody thought I saw. You thought I saw."

He looked at me for a long time before he finally spoke.

"I was wrong," he said. "I'm sorry."

A lot of people were sorry.

Gina came to see me. She cried and said she couldn't believe she had doubted me. She practically begged me to stay friends with her.

Mr. Genovese came to see me. He said he was sorry. He said what I did was very brave and that it meant a lot to Mrs. Genovese and to the rest of the family that the person who had shot Martin was going to be brought to justice. He said he wanted to give me the reward he had offered. I told him I didn't want it, but then my mom talked to him. She said she would put it in a special fund to pay for my education.

Anna Genovese came the day after her father. She said she was sorry too, but I could tell she still blamed me.

I never heard from the Carsons.

TWENTY-FIVE
Kelly

INT.—HOSPITAL HALLWAY—DAY
KELLY is standing in the hall as hospital staff bustle by and patients shuffle up and down the hall in their hospital gowns and robes.

KELLY
(to the camera)
They're discharging Tegan. She's going to have to go to rehab for a while because of the muscle damage to her left shoulder. But the doctor says she can expect a full recovery. Well, a full physical recovery. She's been really quiet since it happened, and she hasn't once said "I told you so." I still can't believe she took a chance like that.

(shaking her head)

It's crazy. She had no idea who the guy was. She'd never seen him before, and Clark never mentioned him. And the guy—he said he didn't realize that there was anyone else in the car, you know, on account of the tinted windows. But nobody believed her. *I* didn't even believe her for a while. Everybody said she must have seen the guy, and if she said she didn't, it was because she was scared. They called her a coward. They treated her like garbage because of it.

The door opens to a room directly across from where KELLY is standing.

MRS. TYRELL'S VOICE

(from inside the room)

Kelly, come and help me with your sister's things.

KELLY

Coming.

(to the camera)

They said she was a coward. They said that of course she'd seen. And because of that, the killer started to get nervous. That's when he knew—or thought—

that there was a witness. That's what Detective Zorbas said. And when Tegan put that video up...

(shakes her head again)

That's the thing, what they call the irony of it. If everyone had believed Tegan when she said she didn't see anything, the guy probably would have got away with it. I mean, I didn't know about Clark keying his van. Anna didn't know about the guy threatening Clark. No one did, because Clark was too embarrassed to say anything about it. But the whole time, he was taking revenge on the guy. According to the guy, his van was keyed *three times*—and one time, just before the shooting, he saw Clark and yelled at him, and Clark ran. But Clark didn't tell anyone about that either. So the guy would have got away with it. No one would ever have figured out he did it. The cops were way off base on the motive. It would have been an unsolved case—except that everyone had their stupid opinion about what must have happened, even though they weren't there. They called Tegan a coward and turned her into an outcast, and she did the only thing she could think of to fight back. That's what solved the case, not crackerjack police work.

MRS. TYRELL'S VOICE
(impatient now)
Kelly!

KELLY sighs as she pushes herself away from the wall she has been leaning on.

KELLY
(to the camera)
Life, huh?
(to her mother)
I'm coming!

She disappears into the hospital room.

THE END

Norah McClintock's fascinating mysteries are hard to put down. She is a five-time winner of the Crime Writers of Canada's Arthur Ellis Award for Best Juvenile Crime Novel. Although Norah is a freelance editor, she still manages to write at least one novel a year. Norah grew up in Montreal, Quebec, and now lives with her family in Toronto, Ontario. This is her eleventh book with Orca. More information about Norah is available at www.web.net/~nmbooks.

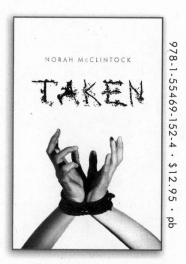

orca soundings

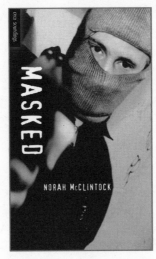

978-1-55469-364-1 $9.95 pb
978-1-55469-365-8 $16.95 lib

WHEN DANIEL ENTERS A CONVENIENCE STORE on a secret mission, he doesn't expect to run into anyone he knows. That would ruin everything. When Rosie shows up, she's hoping to make a quick getaway with her waiting boyfriend. But the next person through the door is wearing a mask and holding a gun. Now things are getting complicated.

"McClintock is a master of mystery and crime...Readers will be drawn into the lives of the characters and gripped with the electric plot and unexpected twists...*Masked* is exceptional in its ability to capture a dramatic and tragically life-changing story for so many characters in little more than 100 pages. Highly Recommended." —*CM Magazine*

orca soundings

978-1-55469-138-8 $9.95 pb
978-1-55469-139-5 $16.95 lib

ETHAN LIVES IN A FOSTER HOME, STRUGGLING
to put his life on the right track. Involved in a photo-
graphy program for at-risk kids, he finds himself
threatened again and again by someone who wants
his camera. What does Ethan know? And what is on his
camera that someone is willing to kill for? Struggling
to stay out of trouble and solve the mystery, he discovers
he has all the answers. He just has to figure out the
questions.

"At just over 100 pages, *Picture This* by Norah McClintock
offers readers an amazing amount of action and mystery.
Ethan is portrayed as the typical at-risk, big-city teen trying
to improve his life. Readers will cheer him on as he works
to hang on to his new life." —*TeensReadToo.com*

orca soundings

978-1-55143-989-1 $9.95 pb
978-1-55143-991-4 $16.95 lib

JOJO'S BACK, AND PEOPLE ARE TENSE AND afraid all over again. Some people just wish Jojo would go away and never come back.

Then there are the people who have hate in their hearts. These people wish something bad would happen to Jojo. Something really bad.

Ardell Withrow is one of those people.

"Bullying and revenge are common themes in young adult literature, but author Norah McClintock gives these classic themes an updated twist...The experiences in the book are ones to which almost any reader will relate."

—*Journal of Adolescent and Adult Literacy*